MIDLIFE MAGIC MALADY

PARANORMAL WOMEN'S FICTION

LEGACY WITCHES OF SHADOW COVE

JENNIFER L. HART

D1526041

ELEMENTS UNLEASHED

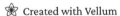

CONTENTS

LEGACY WITCHES OF SHADOW COVE

BOOK 3

Midlife Magic Malady
Hart/ Jennifer L.

1.Women's—Fiction 2. North Carolina—Fiction 3.
Paranormal—Fiction 4. Witch Romance—Fiction 5.
Demons Romance—Fiction 6.Twins—Fiction 7. Small
Towns—Fiction 8. ADHD—Fiction 9. American
Humorous—Fiction 10.Mountain Living —Fiction 11.
Divorce— Fiction 12. Shifter Romance—Fiction I. Title

ISBN 9798868481307

A mysterious illness casts a haunting veil over the residents of Shadow Cove. When hallucinations grip the small town twin sister witches, Bella and Donna Sanders must find the cure. Or die trying.

After Donna's son falls victim to the magical illness, the twins embark on a perilous quest to cure him and the rest of the town. Alongside Bella's mysterious demon love interest, they journey into a lost realm and hunt for a mystical cure. As secrets of their witchy legacy unravel, the twins discover a painful sacrifice may be the only way to escape.

Can the bonds of sisterhood, the power of newfound love, and the legacy of witchcraft prevail? Or will love wither in a prison with no escape?

Midlife Magic Malady is a captivating journey into a world where magic and belief collide and where the true strength of passion is put to the ultimate test. If you enjoy tales of forbidden love, sacrifice, and magic, you will adore Jennifer L. Hart's spellbinding tale. <u>Buy *Midlife Magic Malady* and summon your sense of adventure now!</u>

CONTENT WARNING
SKIP TO AVOID POSSIBLE SPOILERS

This book includes characters dealing with past trauma, sexual assault, sudden violence, themes of PTSD, flashbacks, crude language, and detailed sex on the page.

MIDLIFE MAGIC MALADY

CHAPTER 1
BELLA

Doctor Edgars sat down across the desk from us. She was an elegant woman, almost regal. Her gray hair was pulled back into a severe bun but the skin around her eyes and mouth was unwrinkled. The quintessential silver vixen. Was she even in her fifties? Maybe she was closer to our age, mid-forties. Prematurely gray, it happened to the best of us.

When she spoke all the idle thoughts I'd entertained about her age got bounced out of my head like overzealous drunks at a strip club.

Her voice was smooth and accent-free, like a news broadcaster's as she delivered the verdict. "I've carefully reviewed your answers on the intake paperwork as well as the statements you've made over the past six months, and I do believe you have ADHD, Ms. Sanders."

For the span of a heartbeat, I didn't know which of us she was addressing. Even though my sister had divorced her pantload of a husband, Donna went by her hyphenated married name, Sanders-Allen. I was just Bella. Or witchling to a certain demon. But Donna already knew she had adult attention deficit hyperactive disorder. She had it and dealt with it like a champ.

My twin squeezed my hand. I glanced over to where she sat. Her dark hair was bluntly cut and dyed to raven's wing black, hiding the telltale silver strands that threaded through my hair. Her green eyes drank in my face, as though she waited for a reaction from me.

"What?" I hissed at her.

"Did you hear what she said?" Donna asked as though I were an idiot child.

I might as well be. I'd once been powerful in my space, Storm Grove Manor. The type of creature with whom one did not fuck. In a bland doctor's office with austere décor and strange scents, with the sounds of ringing phones and the indistinct chatter from the television carrying in from the waiting area, I was totally out of my element.

The sentence had been delivered. The question *what the hell is wrong with me* finally had an answer. I shrugged in what I hoped was a nonchalant way. "We knew it was a possibility."

Donna deflated right before my eyes. What had she been expecting? For me to break down into tears? She ought to know me better. I never showed weakness to any potential enemy. And even though Dr. Edgars was "just trying to help," I didn't trust her enough to let my guard down.

Donnan turned back to the doctor. On her lap sat a yellow legal pad and I saw her glance down at it, checking over the questions she intended to ask.

"Does she need medication, do you think? She's still nursing her twins, so we're concerned about possible side effects...."

I turned my head and stared out the window at the naked tree branches, the dormant brown grass, and the wet pavement of the parking lot reserved for medical professionals. I didn't tell Donna that I wasn't concerned. It didn't matter if the doctor gave me medicine. I wouldn't take it. Magic was in my blood, not medications. The solution to my problems wouldn't be found in this sterile space.

I loved my sister, but we were two entirely different people. She could cling to her mundane solutions, but I wasn't about to ignore my legacy.

"...unnecessary at this time." When I tuned back into the conversation, Dr. Edgars was shaking her head. "I think the wiser course of action is to track your day-to-day, Bella. See where you're struggling and try to come up with solutions that work for you."

"That's exactly what I intend to do. Thank you for your help, Doctor. We truly appreciate it." I clapped my hands on my knees and rose.

"But...?" Donna's brows pulled together, and she shot a panicked glance at her list.

"Come on, Donna. We've taken up enough of the doctor's time." I stared directly at her and could tell by the way she stiffened in the seat that my eyes had turned to mirrors. Reflection was my innate magical ability and though I finessed my powers in ways Donna couldn't, there were times when the leash that held it in check slipped.

Donna reached over the desk, offering her hand, thanking the doctor as though I hadn't just done the same. Not waiting for her, I followed the red arrows around the corner and past the receptionist's desk, uninterested in making a follow-up appointment.

We had what we'd come to get—Donna's precious answer. It changed nothing.

The North Carolina sun beat down on my uncovered head. The air was mild and unseasonably warm for February in the mountains. I headed to my 1970 jade green coup Deville, fishing the keys out of the deep pockets of my broomstick purple skirt. Too bad it wasn't convertible weather. At least I hadn't been forced to ride in Donna's ugly little Impala. There was only so much indignity a witch could tolerate in one day.

"What the shit, Bells?" Donna started in on me as soon as she slammed the passenger's side door.

I winced theatrically. "Don't take your rage issues out on my ride."

She pivoted her upper body in the seat until she looked me dead in the eye. "You just waltzed out of there like nothing had changed."

"Nothing has changed," I ground out. "I went in there with ADHD and left with it. So, everything is exactly the same as before."

I inserted the key and turned. The motor sputtered and choked but didn't catch. I tried again. Nothing.

"Donna," I growled.

Her hands flew up. "It's not me, I swear!"

I lowered my sunglasses so I could glare at her over the brim. "Oh really? You're pissed that we're leaving and suddenly my car, which was working perfectly well this morning, won't start, thereby making it impossible for us to leave? Whether you're doing it intentionally or not, it's you and your comeuppance. Damn it!" I slammed my hands down on the wheel.

We sat in silence for a beat, each of us lost in our own thoughts. Donna's hand propped up her chin, her expression lost.

She spoke first. "I thought it would help."

"Really? You thought breaking my car would help?" I scoffed.

She shook her head. "Getting a diagnosis let me understand what was going on in my wonky brain. It guided me in the right direction. It helped me accept myself as I am, my strengths and weaknesses. It helped combat things that were counterproductive so I could achieve my goals. I want that for you."

My head thumped against the leather headrest. "Look, I get it. And I appreciate that you were trying to help me. That you're always trying to fix things for me. But I'm not broken, Donna. Neither of us are."

She worried her lower lip. "Aren't we?"

I grasped her hand in mine. "No. I get that this was a big deal for you. You're a

professional organizer, you like your labels."

She snorted.

"But I'm different. I'm used to living on the fringes of what you deem polite society. I go

to sleep to the sound of werewolves howling and bats scrabbling around in the attic. A demon is converting our ancestral home into a Gothic Inn. What's the point of dwelling on the things about me that don't work as society expects when I've already rejected society?"

Donna let out a weary sigh. "So, all the research I've been doing for your benefit? All the conversations we've had. What was the point?"

I shrugged. "Did it make you feel better, hearing that we're two peas in a neurodivergent pod?"

The corner of her mouth kicked up. "Kinda."

"Then that's the point." I squeezed her hand once and then let go. "It still doesn't get us out of this parking lot. Matilda Longshanks needs to leave by five to get to her coven meeting."

Matilda Longshanks was a local Healer. She belonged to a coven that met a few towns east of Shadow Cove. I'd enlisted her help to babysit the twins, Ember and Astrid, while we went to see the mortal doctors. There were no rideshares in town and the twin's car seats were in the back of the DeVille.

Donna rolled her head along the backrest to look at me. "Well, I have an idea. But you're not going to like it."

I stared at her for a beat. "You can't be serious."

"Come on, Bells. You know he'll drop whatever he's doing to come get you."

She wasn't wrong. I'd been avoiding Declan, aka my landlord, aka the demon that had tricked me out of my ancestral home, as much as I possibly could. When he stopped by to see the progress at Storm Grove, I took the twins to the werewolf bunkhouse or into town—anything to avoid that burning midnight gaze that haunted my dreams.

"How are you so blasé about asking for a favor from a demon?" I snapped at my sister.

She shrugged. "Who else can we call? You don't have a personal assistant anymore and there is *literally* no one else who will go out of their way for the witches of Shadow Cove."

"We could move," I offered. I'd had the thought more than once over the past six months, though I'd never broached the subject with my sister.

"Huh?" she blinked at me.

"Can you imagine it? We could just pack up the twins and go somewhere where no one knows who we are or what we can do." No more fearful or hateful looks from the citizens I'd devoted my life to protecting. No more legacy to live up to. It sounded like absolute freedom.

"You would never leave Storm Grove," Donna sighed. Before I could protest, she added, "And to tell you the truth, I wouldn't either even if the town sucks canal water backward. Now quit stalling and call him."

I huffed out a breath. "I want you to remember this the next time you call me unreasonably stubborn."

Donna gave me a little finger wave as I exited the car and scrolled through my contacts until I hit the Ds for dickhead demon. It took very little time since I had only about a dozen contacts. People avoided me like the plague. I really should consider moving.

"Well, well, witchling," the melodic voice crooned into the line, wrapping me in dark silk. "It's been a while since you reached out. Are you finally prepared to give in to our undeniable chemistry?"

"No." I bit the word out. "My car broke down and

Donna and I need a ride. Could you send someone... please?" I tacked on the last word, so it didn't come across as a demand between demon summoner and summoned demon. I'd used that tone with him before. It didn't feel right though, not since things had changed between us. *Never should have let him kiss me.*

"You beg so nicely, witchling," the demon crooned. "How can I say no?"

If I kept this level of stress going my molars would be ground to dust by the end of the month. "So, you'll send someone?"

"For a price."

Always the price. "What is it you want?"

He let out a long breath. "A conversation with you minus the buffer of your offspring or that overprotective twin of yours."

I was about to tell him that we had nothing to discuss that couldn't be said in front of Donna or my children. But a demon's first offer was typically the best a witch could get. "Fine. Stick around after I put the twins down for the night and we can have a conversation."

At Storm Grove, on my turf. The center of my power and a reminder of who I was and what Declan was.

Anything else was just too risky.

DONNA and her adopted werewolf Joseline took the babies out to the conservatory the instant we'd returned home. I'd told her about Declan's bargain and while she hadn't approved, she didn't try to talk me out of it either.

"Ask for the manor back," Donna had urged. "I'm sure he'd give it to you if you asked him for it."

"It's not that simple." Nothing ever was when it came to demonic bargains. Declan, for goddess alone knew what reason, wanted Storm Grove. He'd dumped tens of thousands into our ancestral home over the past several months. No matter that Donna insisted the demon had a soft spot for me in his coal-black heart. He was a businessman and would expect a return on his investment.

Just the thought of that gave me a hot flash. Which was a problem.

Back in the beginning, when I'd first summoned him, my fear had kept my crazy attraction in check. When had that changed? When he'd helped me tend my newborns? Or the day he'd taken me out for ice cream? Or was it when he'd shared a few insights into life in the demonic underworld?

Whatever had prompted the change one thing was clear—he was dangerous to my peace of mind.

Declan was dangerous, period. My fear of him had transmuted into fear of how he made me feel.

Normally I would have dragged him into the kitchen. Unfortunately, the kitchen was the center of the current renovation storm. All the old appliances were gone, walls had been knocked down and wires poked through the four-by-six beams. Instead, I gestured into the parlor.

The space was dusty, more from disuse than the free-floating plaster particles that littered the lower floor of the manor despite Donna's best efforts. The demon strode into the room and swiped a finger across the antique cherry desk. "We need to get you a new house-keeper, witchling. This place isn't habitable as it is."

"It's fine," I insisted, ignoring his use of the word we. I wasn't about to take any more favors from the demon. "We'll clean it up after the renovation is done. What is it you wanted to discuss?"

Hair black as a raven's wing fell rakishly across his forehead. "I want you to be my date to a certain event. Hear me out," he added.

I shook my head. "I don't think that's a good idea."

Declan strode closer. His black eyes were so dark they didn't distinguish between iris and pupil as he searched my features. "Why not? Are you afraid to be alone with me?"

"Of course not." I lifted my chin and prayed he wouldn't be able to hear the rapid beat of my heart. It would give away the lie.

Declan turned toward the window. The days were creeping up and there was still a little light outside, enough to kiss the evergreens with a tangy orange hue. "This isn't personal. I need your particular ability for a business arrangement."

He meant my power of reflection. I crossed my arms over my chest. "Really? You found someone you can't bribe or bargain into submission?"

"Someone other than you, witchling?" The corner of his mouth kicked up. "Despite what you may think I try to keep my business dealings on the level. In this partic-ular instance, the person I'm dealing with is cagey. I can't get a read on what it is he wants. I want you to read him for me. That way I'll know where I can apply pressure most effectively."

I opened my mouth to say no again when he stepped forward. Long fingers covered my lips and his dark eyes sparked as he whispered. "And in return for your assistance, I'll let you look at any of the forbidden scrolls in my inner sanctum."

I swallowed hard—demon magic. I'd used it once. And I'd never felt so powerful. My hands balled into fists at my side. I wanted to say no. An evening out with the demon, even if it was only a business meeting, was a bad idea.

But the way that power snagged my soul, blown through all the cold corners of my body and lit a fire in my heart.... I wanted to feel that again.

My gaze dropped to the cord around Declan's neck. I'd never seen what sort of charm he wore on it, but it was always there, a small lump in the middle of his chest.

"When?" I breathed.

His mouth curved into a wicked smile, and I tried not to flinch.

"Tomorrow night. And dress sexy."

CHAPTER 2
DONNA

"What the hell am I even doing?" I whispered into the dark room. I lay in bed. Not my bed, where Joseline was sprawled curled up in wolf form. Even with keen werewolf ears, the girl was a sound sleeper. She didn't stir when I slipped out of bed and padded across the hall into Axel's room. Well, technically it wasn't his room anymore. All the rooms belonged to Declan. But unlike the other rooms that were remodeled for guests, this one was exactly how the fury had left it.

After sliding between the cool, crisp sheets, I curled up on the pillow that no longer smelled like spring rain and ozone because it had been six freaking months since he'd slept on this bed.

I'd never got a chance to share it with him. Or invite him into mine.

Six months I'd waited for him to return. He called when he could, which wasn't often enough to suit me. He never told me where he was. According to the furies, it was safer for me if I didn't know. And though I loved hearing his voice, he never spoke the words my heart yearned to hear.

That he was coming back to me.

A month in, I'd been disappointed, but unsurprised. After the last phone call, I was beginning to think he would never come back to Storm Grove.

Which lead my wonky brain in a circle back to the beginning. Wondering what the hell I was doing.

Could I keep my life on hold while Axel sorted himself out? What if it took years to find a way to control his inner fury? Decades even? He was young, younger than me by a solid two decades. He had time.

I was in the second phase of my adult life. Freshly divorced with my only son off at college. I was supposed to be taking advantage of this time, not cooling my heels in my family's ancestral home, waiting for the phone to ring like some forlorn high school girl. I knew better than this.

But the sad reality was that I didn't want anything else for myself. I wanted to help Bella, even though she'd made it clear that she didn't need me. An ADHD diagnosis had changed nothing for her. For me, it had been like a breath of fresh air after a long, cold winter. The promise of a better tomorrow.

Sure, I was helping with the twins. Ember and Astrid were incredible, and I loved every second with my niece and nephew. It reminded me of when Devon was a baby. I spent hours playing this little piggy and watching him blow spit bubbles. Those were memories no one could take away. But a witch couldn't live in her memories. She needed to find a path to walk. I thought mine would be with Axel.

I was beginning to believe I'd been too hasty.

A light tap sounded on the door. "Donna? You in there?"

"Yeah." After scrubbing my pajama sleeve over my eyes, I sat up in bed.

Bella pushed the door open and hesitated at the threshold. "What are you doing in here?"

I shrugged. "Couldn't sleep."

Her expression softened. With the full moon illuminating a path on the floor I could make out her curved figure, swathed in a thick robe, though her feet were bare. She held a baby monitor in one hand and through it I could hear the soft steady sounds of the twins breathing.

An owl hooted and both of us turned our heads toward the sound. An owl meant impending change. Fricking perfect.

Bella rolled her eyes. "Just what we needed, more upheaval."

"What did Declan want?" I asked her.

Instead of perching on the side of the bed, she dragged a rocking chair out of the corner and curled up in it. I tossed her a blanket so she could cover her legs. "He wants me to go with him to an event tomorrow night."

Both my eyebrows shot up to my hairline. "Really?"

She nodded. "I'm supposed to use Reflection to read a potential seller for him."

Sounded simple enough. Bella used magic all the time. "And you agreed?"

"It seemed like the easiest way to bank future favors from him."

Future favors, like getting Storm Grove turned over to our family? Bella didn't seem nearly as eager to get the matter settled as I was. Weird, since she'd lived here her whole life. I would have thought she'd put up more of a fight.

Her gaze drifted to the nightstand, to where I'd set my phone. "Have you heard from Axel?"

I exhaled a weary sigh. "No."

She rocked forward in the chair, bracing one foot on the floor to hold it steady, and reached out for my hand. "You must miss him."

"Yeah." A lump formed in my throat. "But I'm sort of wondering if this isn't for the best."

"What do you mean?" Bella narrowed her emerald eyes at me and then sat back. "Do not tell me that now you're seeing sense about that fury."

I glared at her. "Shut up."

She laughed and it was a hollow sound. "Donna, you are so damn stubborn, you know that?"

"Pot," I pointed at her and then chucked a thumb at my chest. "Meet kettle."

She let out a sigh. "Okay, so even though I still think he's incredibly dangerous and all wrong for you for a multitude of reasons, up to and including that he let you die in your past life—"

I flinched.

"I still think it's your insecurity talking."

15

I ran a hand through my hair. "How long am I supposed to wait, Bells? My life is on hold here. I haven't taken on a new client in months."

"You're working for the demon. Goddess knows he's a handful."

I narrowed my gaze at her. "Why don't you use his name?"

"Um, because he gets really pissed when I call him Az—"

I held up a hand. "Not his summoning name. You're always calling him *the demon*. Like you need to remind yourself of what he is or something."

"Like I could forget," she scoffed. "Tell you what, Donna. You sort out your own messy love life and leave me to mine."

I grinned. "Ah, so you're admitting that you have feelings for him!"

"I'm not—" She was cut off by the sound of a cranky wail through the baby monitor. "Saved by the midnight feeding," I teased.

She rose and stretched. At the door, she hesitated. "Aren't you worried about me being with the demon?"

"No." I lifted my chin. "Because the bastard knows that if he hurts you I will end him, comeuppance style."

Bella laughed as I'd intended and then shut the door behind her.

I resettled on the bed and tried to go to sleep. After fifteen minutes, I gave up, snapped the bedside light on, and reached for my phone.

In the notes section, I pulled up the plans I'd been listing out for Axel's food truck. I'd been researching start-up costs as well as the market here in Shadow Cove. Ideally, he would be set to open shortly after Mother's Day weekend and be positioned to make money during the busy tourist season. Florida seemed to empty out that time of year and come to the high country with money to burn. I had numbers for the demon and Declan had agreed to look over my business plan. We all knew Axel could cook. But would he be back to Shadow Cove by then?

Would he even still want to open a food truck? I'd been too nervous to ask. Because if he'd changed his mind about that dream, maybe he'd changed his mind about me.

Past lives be damned. We needed to live in this one. Having one divorce under my belt had taught me that forever wasn't always as long as it sounded.

Irritated, I closed the phone, snapped off the light, and willed my wonky brain to shut the hell up.

It didn't listen. I spent the night replaying every single interaction I'd had with Axel since the day we'd met.

Goddess help me, I missed him.

"No," I kvetched into the phone cradled between my ear and shoulder as I scanned the order. "I ordered the black double ovens, not the cream ones."

"It says on the order, cream" the man with the thick

southern accent drawled. Not North Carolina. Georgia or maybe Alabama.

"Well, the sheet I have matches your online catalog," I argued. "And I have the serial number for the black right here. Zero zero seven—"

"Hold a moment ma'am." The bored customer service rep put me on hold before I could rattle off the rest of the number.

"Bastards, all of you." I tried to think of an appropriate comeuppance for customer service reps who put people on hold hoping they'd give up instead of just admitting there was a fricking problem. Traffic jams maybe. Why was it so difficult for people to own their shit instead of blame-shifting? The cream ovens were still workable, just not with a gothic kitchen.

The sound of sawing, and hammering drifted into the conservatory from said kitchen. Footsteps sounded overhead along with the blare of a radio as the back bedrooms on the second floor were renovated. I rose and shut the door, not wanting the twins to be disturbed from their mid-morning nap. Bella was down at the bunkhouse with the werewolves, and I was doing double duty, babysitting, and trying to get our kitchen up and running.

I wished my sister had seen me when I realized about the ovens. I'd been ready to hit the ceiling over the error, but Declan had told me to simply order new ones in my preferred color as though it was no biggie to eat thousands of dollars of wrong equipment.

The demon was investing in Storm Grove Manor. And I knew it was about more than opening a gothic-style B&B. And I knew it because of the single slip he'd made when we were first going over the design.

I could still see the flare of fire in his eyes as he murmured, "I trust your taste, Donna Sanders-Allen. You know what she needs."

She. Not the customers. I knew what Bella needed.

He was setting Storm Grove up to generate income for her. So Bella would have a way to provide for her twins. And he knew that I would design spaces for her to do her magic, to raise her children.

I'd started by decluttering. It had been a huge job, emptying those back bedrooms of centuries' worth of Sanders' clutter. Old steamer trunks filled with moth-eaten clothing, paintings of people I didn't recognize, dusty records, and broken furniture.

It had been cathartic. At first, I'd worried Bella would want to hold on to some of the rubbish. But she'd been oddly indifferent. She'd even helped me haul stuff to the donation centers, the dump, and the antique store that agreed to sell on commission. Even the old linens found a home at the local animal shelter. Each load I'd hauled out of the Manor had made me feel lighter. Bella seemed easier too. Clutter made ADHD symptoms worse. A busy environment provoked a busy mind, so my goal was to make the manor a dark sanctuary for my sister as well as the potential guests.

Declan approved it all with little fuss. The intense looks Declan gave Bella when her back was turned didn't go unnoticed. That ride in the car with the two of them had been excruciating. Though I couldn't believe it, I was rooting for him. In business, he was so confident. With magic, he came off as almost arrogant. But with my sister, Declan seemed almost...shy. It was endearing. My gut told me he'd be good for Bella if she ever gave him a shot.

A flash of light caught my eye. Frowning, I turned and spotted a familiar silver Prius wending its way up the long drive to the manor house.

It couldn't be. My heart thudded. The twins were strapped into their double stroller, but the wind was whipping, and I didn't want them to catch a chill. Instead, I picked up the baby monitor and slipped out the door to the patio where all the outdoor furniture was carefully swaddled for the winter, and around the side of the house.

He parked right in front of the main entrance, seven steps down from where Bonnie and Clyde, the gargoyles slumbered. A squeal escaped as his long lanky frame unfolded from behind the wheel and I ran for him.

"Devon!" I shouted. He'd been by at Christmas to meet his new cousins, though because of the chaos of renovations he had stayed with his father in the house where he'd grown up. I hadn't seen anywhere near enough of my son and his sudden arrival filled me with delight.

His dimple flashed and he reached out an arm to embrace me as I rushed up to him.

"What are you doing here?" I asked when I finally pulled away. "It's not spring break yet, is it?"

He shook his head. "Nah."

I stepped back and searched his face, waiting for an explanation.

Devon had taken the best features from the Sanders and Allen lines. My green eyes and dark hair, and Lewis's height as well as the athletic build he'd had in high school. Despite the cold his skin was tanned, and muscles bulged beneath his t-shirt. He must have been making good use of the school's gym facilities before soccer started.

He rubbed the back of his neck and avoided eye contact. "See, the thing is I sort of left school."

"Obviously." He was attending a state university several hours away on a soccer scholarship. "For how long?"

He met my gaze and held it. "For good. I'm dropping out."

CHAPTER 3
BELLA

"Come out and show me or I'm coming in to see," Donna warned.

"How long is Devon here for?" I asked as I made a face. Side boob spilled out from the slinky purple fabric in an almost obscene way.

"I have no idea. And don't change the subject!" Donna's tone was all sharp and mom-like, as it had been since her son had arrived on our doorstep. "Does the dress work?"

"I don't know," I groused as I turned to look at the back of my dress in the mirror. "It's threading a thin line between sexy and trashy."

"Let me be the judge," Donna insisted.

When it came to clothing, Donna's taste ran more conservative than my own. If I was in doubt, she'd put the kibosh on it in a heartbeat. That would be just the excuse I needed to call off the evening.

My fingers itched to unroll those demon scrolls and find the secrets hidden within. I felt the same way when reading a phenomenal book series. Addictive, almost like a high. Dopamining, Donna called the constant craving for another hit of euphoric goodness.

Squaring my shoulders and lifting my chin, I sauntered out from the mirror alcove. Donna had been lying on her side on the rug with Astrid and Ember having tummy time. She blinked up at me. I paused directly in front of three sets of Sanders green eyes and then pivoted in a circle. Astrid gurgled and Ember reached for his toes and passed gas.

"So that's what they think. How about you?" I did a pirouette, so she got the full effect.

"It's perfect," Donna breathed.

"You're kidding." I gestured to my chest. "Do you not see the enormous amount of side boob on display?"

"You've got nursing mom boobs going on," Donna said. "Might as well smoke 'em while you've got 'em. Once these two are weened, they'll deflate like dollar store balloons." She gestured to her own chest.

I snorted, but insecurity bubbled up. "You're sure I look okay?"

"You look more than okay." Donna rose with fluid grace and fussed with the halter straps that twisted around my neck then gave my bare shoulders a reassuring squeeze. "You look terrific. Hot enough to incinerate a demon."

The front doorbell rang.

"Speak of the devil, and he shall appear." Donna grinned. "Want me to get it and torment him while you make him wait?"

"Nah. Better if we get this shitshow on the road." I

picked up the black shawl embroidered with silver ivy and swung it around my bare shoulders before sliding my stocking feet into purple pumps.

My heels clicked on the stone floor, echoing through the three-story atrium and bouncing off the curved stone stairs as I made my way to the door. *Not a date,* I told myself. This was not a date. Even if getting dolled up for the demon felt like a date. Squaring my shoulders, I took a deep breath and then turned the knob, half hiding behind the massive door.

The demon lounged on the other side. A dark god in a tux with ebony locks falling forward to give him a roguish charm. He was already up on his high horse, his expression irritated. "About time, witchling. I don't want to arrive—"

Our gazes locked. I lifted my chin and waited while he gave me a slow scan up and then down and back. I got the feeling that he took note of everything, from the height of my heels to the fringe on my wrap, to the elegant chignon Donna had wrestled my hair into. A few tendrils had already escaped and were curling around my face.

Fire burned in those black irises, making me shiver.

"You were saying?" I couldn't help but needle him.

"Damned if I can remember." He reached forward and unclasped my hand from where it had been gripping the door. He spun me in a slow circle and whistled low. "You're scrumptious, Bella Sanders."

The compliment warmed me. I hadn't dressed up to go out in almost a year. Pregnancy had wreaked havoc on my figure, expanding things to almost obscene proportions. After the credit card mess I'd gotten myself into, Donna only let me buy vintage discount clothing that was usually covered in baby spit-up. The combined look made me feel frumpy and unkempt. Even if I didn't want the demon, I wasn't above basking in a little male appreciation. It was just the ego boost a single mom needed.

It had nothing to do with the way those dark eyes devoured me as though I was the main course in a feast he'd been eagerly anticipating. Not a thing.

"Let me just say goodbye to the twins." I pulled free of his grip and if there was a little extra sway in my hips as I headed down the hall to where Donna was surely watching us, well, who could blame me?

Donna snapped the magical compact shut. "Not to be all I told you so but, hot damn, Bella. That demon wants you. Bad."

"He can wait until the end of time." I bent down and blew a raspberry on Ember's pudgy belly making him giggle and then dropped a soft kiss on Astrid's cheek. "You two behave for Aunt Donna, okay?"

"Have fun." Donna passed me the compact with a sly grin. "Just so you know I'm not watching."

"Shall we go?" I prompted as I approached the demon. "I'd hate for you to be late."

Declan extended his elbow in an old-fashioned gesture. I took it and let him lead me down the steps to the waiting black Porche Cayenne.

"Where's your SUV?" I asked as he held the door for me.

"At the hotel. This is more in line with the image I want to present tonight." He waited until I was tucked securely into the sumptuous leather seat, also black, before shutting the door and rounding the front of the vehicle. I stole a few glances as he settled his six-foot-two frame behind the wheel. I wanted to tell him he looked fantastic but feared he'd take it the wrong way. No matter that this felt like a date. It wasn't. I needed to remember that.

Taking a deep breath, I enjoyed the aroma of new car, the most expensive smell on the planet. It was only then that I realized what was missing.

"No sulfur," I murmured to Declan with wonder.

"It's been weeks since I used magic. I told you the brimstone fades. Do I smell passably human?"

Before I could think better of it, I leaned into his body and drew a deep breath. He smelled like an orgasm waiting to happen. I bit off the words and simply nodded.

"Good." He turned the key and the Porche purred to life.

"Tell me about the target," I asked. Business. This was a business deal for him. And for me too, so I could get my greedy hands on those demonic scrolls.

Declan slid me a look before refocusing on the road. "If that's the way you want it, witchling."

I bobbed my head. "It is."

THE EVENT WAS BEING HELD at one of the swankier ski resorts in our area. Even the views from Storm Grove hadn't prepared me for the floor-to-ceiling windows that overlooked the little village below, the blankets of artificially manufactured snow that covered the slopes, encouraging people to come frolic in the winter wonderland and pay hard-earned money to do it. Behind me, people in evening wear milled about while a string quartet played Vivaldi's Four Seasons.

Not my typical Saturday night.

Even better in this setting, no one knew my identity. I wasn't the infamous witch of Shadow Cove. Instead, I could pass myself off as an elegant woman on the arm of a wealthy benefactor of whatever charity was being sponsored tonight. A world apart from Storm Grove Manor, witchcraft that I wasn't using, and the stress of single motherhood.

No wonder I didn't feel like myself.

"Ever been skiing?" Declan plucked two champagne flutes off the tray of a passing waiter. He offered me a glass. My shawl had been left at coat check and the sleeve of his jacket came perilously close to brushing my side boob. I held my breath but there was no contact as I took the glass.

"No. Sledding and snow tubing only." I took a sip. The champagne was cool and crisp, the bubbles bursting on my tongue, teasing my taste buds to a new level of alertness. I took another sip and another until the glass was empty. "Donna found our old toboggan in the attic. The two of us used to drag it up the hill behind the lake and then ride down to that big open field." The memory made me smile.

Declan's lips twitched. "Will you do that with the twins?"

"They're a little young for it," I explained. "When they're older for sure."

He nodded as though taking in important information. Which he was. It was hard for me to remember that Declan hadn't had a typical childhood. Instead, he'd been battling for survival in the demon arena.

Oblivious to my thoughts, he plucked the nearly empty flute from my hand and set it on a nearby table before extending a hand. "Our target is on the far side of the room. Care to dance?"

I took his hand. Though I wanted to admit I wasn't much of a dancer, the aftereffects of the champagne made my head and consequently my entire body feel lighter. Declan spun me in a slow circle before drawing me close. I let him lead. He did so with grace, waltzing us across the floor. His palms warmed the bare skin of my back and it felt only natural to look up into his dark eyes and wait until he gave me a signal.

"We're going to get him alone," the demon crooned as he checked the progress of the target across the room. "That way you can do your thing."

"My thing?" I felt dazed.

The corner of his mouth kicked up. "Champagne went right to your head, didn't it?" Those dark irises flicked down to my mouth when I wet suddenly dry lips.

"I didn't eat anything today." Nerves had gotten the better part of me. "And it's been over a year since I had alcohol."

He made a tut-tutting sound. "Nursing mothers need more calories, not less, witchling."

"I hadn't expected to drink." My tone was defensive.

I'd have to pump and dump for the next twenty-four hours. Good thing there was a reserve of milk in the industrial-sized freezer at the manor. A freezer Declan had bought along with a generator to make sure it would work even if the winter storms took out the power.

"Don't go getting your hackles up," he murmured. "I'm not criticizing you, witchling. And I promise I'll feed you whatever you want as soon as the job is done. And here's our host now."

I turned in his arms and met the gaze of an older gentleman in his late sixties with a snowy white beard and twinkling blue eyes. He was dressed like a cowboy who'd stumbled across a gold mine, complete with a pristine white Stetson.

I glanced from this white hat to Declan's alarmingly dark hair. They depicted quintessential good and evil.

"Mr. Cotter. May I introduce you to my date, Bella Sanders? Bella runs one of my properties for me."

"Is that right?" Cotter's thick Texas drawl matched his hat and bolo tie. "Mind if I steal this pretty lady for a dance?"

Declan stepped back and waved the path toward me. "She's all yours."

My gaze caught him and held for an endless moment. Was it my imagination or did a muscle jump in his jaw? As though the words bothered him on a visceral level.

Shaking my head and brightening my smile I focused on Bill Cotter. Declan had given me the rundown on our way here, but I wanted to assess the man for myself before I went spelunking into his inner secrets.

"So how long you been with our boy, there?" Cotter was nowhere near as smooth a dancer as Declan. Something about the way he moved made me think he was more comfortable on horseback than in a crowded ballroom.

"Pretty much from the day he arrived in town," I smiled.

"And you trust him?" Cotter asked.

Not as far as I can throw him. Of course, I couldn't say that out loud. I was supposed to be helping Declan secure this property, not sabotaging his efforts with the pesky truth. "Well, he's already done so many things with my family's ancestral home. Staying true to the nature of the old Gothic Manor house while upgrading amenities. My sister is helping with the design so it's really a family venture."

Cotter's bushy white brows pulled together. "That's different from what I've heard. He bought this place out on the coast and well, from everything I hear employee turnover is higher than it ought to be. That was a family-run operation, too."

Digging down deep I pulled my magic to the foreground. I captured his gaze, and his lips formed an o of surprise. He was seeing into himself, his reflection displayed in my eyes. "What is it you're worried about when it comes to selling this property, Mr. Cotter?'

"My grandson," he responded right away. "I promised I'd leave him this place."

"And does he want it? Or would he rather have the money from the sale to pursue his own dreams?" I knew

30

the answer. So did Cotter. He just needed a little push to admit it.

"He wants the money. He doesn't care for the cold."

I squeezed his bicep gently. "Then maybe it's your dream for him to inherit this place. Even if it isn't the best thing for him."

We'd stopped moving. All around us, other people danced but the two of us were still. I waited until I felt Cotter stiffen and then step back.

"I'm sorry," he began, shaking off the last tendrils of my influence. "Something's come up. If you'll excuse me."

"Of course. I was just going to grab something to eat." I gestured toward the buffet table.

Still shaky, Cotter moved off at a pace I guessed was far faster than his typical mosey. I could feel Declan's dark gaze on me but made my way to the buffet table, picked up a plate, and perused the spread. Barbecue was the name of the game. Texas-style brisket as well as Carolina vinegar-based. I made a face. Nothing wrong with barbecue but not while wearing fancy clothes. Bypassing the main course, I chose a fruit cabob and several slices of pale cheese. When I turned, Declan stood before me, taking up massive amounts of space, his dark eyes glittering with impatience.

"Well?"

"You'll have your ski resort." I circled past him hunting for a place to sit. The light floaty feeling from the champagne had gone. In its place...guilt maybe? I'd killed a man's dream of legacy. While Declan and the grandson might appreciate it, I wasn't convinced I'd done the right thing.

Declan caught my arm, his gaze searching my face. "You're upset?"

My teeth sank into my lower lip, and I shrugged one shoulder.

He swore and took the plate from my hand.

"Hey," I snapped. "I was going to eat that."

"No, you were going to pick at it and brood. Come on, witchling. I'll feed you a real meal."

I had no choice but to let him lead me out of the ballroom.

Almost an hour later the Porche purred to a stop in front of Declan's hotel. He climbed out and tossed the keys to the valet, before opening my door.

"You should have just taken me home," I said.

He didn't answer, instead tugging me up the steps, past the check-in desk, and through the main dining room, which was swept and shut down for the night. He pushed through a swinging door. I blinked as he flicked on the overhead light, exposing a blindingly white kitchen.

Declan guided me to a stool that sat opposite the large refrigerator. "Sit," he commanded.

"I'm not a dog," I snapped.

He braced his hands on the counter. "Do you want to argue? Or would you prefer if I made you a pesto grilled cheese?"

I blinked. "How did you know that was my favorite?"

"Your former PA." The demon turned and began pulling items out of the fridge. A jar of pesto, and fresh mozzarella. From a basket in one cabinet, he retrieved olive oil, sourdough bread, and a perfectly ripe tomato, the likes of which I hadn't seen since the end of September.

I watched as he poured a drizzle of olive oil onto the pan, adjusted the flame, and then began spreading pesto onto the bread. "He informed me that if you were ever in a bad mood, this was the cure."

I didn't know how I felt about the fury and the demon exchanging notes about my food preferences, but then he slid the golden gooey sandwich in front of me.

The pesto mingled perfectly with the smooth mozzarella and the tomato gave the entire thing that pop of freshness.

I looked from the sandwich to the demon and back.

"Eat, witchling. We'll sort out the rest after."

Knowing good advice when I heard it, I picked up one of the perfectly cut triangles and took a bite.

Sinful decadence. I couldn't help but wonder what the price would be for it.

CHAPTER 4
DONNA

Rapping my knuckles lightly on the door to Axel's —now Devon's—room, I offered him a small smile. "You hungry?"

He squinted at me and then pulled an earbud out. "What did you say?"

"I asked if you were hungry." My smile grew forced.

"I'm good." He made to put the earbud back in, shutting me out.

"Wait, Devon. We need to talk." I stepped into the room, hands outstretched.

"About what?"

His tone rankled. What was it with late teen sons that they could make their middle-aged parents feel like bumbling idiots? Or maybe it was just me. My unique brand of ADHD came with rejection sensitivity dysphoria. In basic terms, I sometimes perceived rejection that wasn't there and often overreacted to it. Devon's not staying with me over Christmas break had felt like a rejection. So did not hearing from Axel. Not seeing him or breathing in his unique spring rain and ozone scent felt like a punishment, like he'd abandoned me. Knowing that this too was just part of how my wonky brain worked helped me not turn into a crying, babbling mess —most of the time. Axel was gone and logically I understood why. Devon was here though, and I needed to find out why.

"About what's going on with you." I sat on the edge of the bed. "You were so excited to go off to school. What changed?"

He wouldn't hold my gaze. "Nothing."

"Nothing," I repeated. "You realize that you're flushing your soccer scholarship over nothing?"

He shrugged.

I reached out and tried to take his hand. "Talk to me."

Devon snatched his hand back. "Like the way you talked to me when you left Dad?"

My hackles rose. "I explained that he'd changed the locks when I was dropping you off at school?"

I'd left some of the grislier details out of the retelling. Like the fact that when I'd broken into said house and caught Lewis *in flagrante delicto* with another woman, he'd had me arrested. Some things my son didn't need to know about his biological father. Even if said father was a colossal hemorrhoid.

I tried again. "If you want to talk about the divorce, we can talk."

"Mom, I'm good. I know you and Dad didn't have the best marriage." He shrugged. "Not like it was a state secret or anything."

I'd always been honest with my son. Maybe too

honest in an oversharing kinda way. He knew I'd smoked pot in college, that I'd dropped out because of my ADHD. He knew that even though organizing and decluttering was a struggle for me it was one of the few skills that made me feel like a real grown-up person, not just an oversized kid stumbling through life. My lists and systems helped me stay focused and mostly, stick to a schedule.

My confessions had been a source of pride. Now I had to wonder if my openness had been a mistake. Did my son respect me for my struggles? Or did he see me as weak?

I scratched an eyebrow. "Okay, so if it's not the divorce then what's up?"

"Nothing. God, can you just leave me be?"

"No, Devon. I can't. I need to know what's going on in your head. You're saying college isn't for you anymore. Why?"

"If you came to see me, you'd know," he muttered.

I sat on the edge of the bed. "I told you I couldn't get away. Your aunt Bella needed me."

"And that's another thing. Since when is she my Aunt Bella?" Devon asked.

"Um, since she's my twin?"

"Yeah, but you never hung out with her. Never brought me up here. In fact, I remember you telling me that we were better off without her. And now all of a sudden you're living here with her? I thought you hated this place."

"I did—"

He didn't let me finish. "Right up until you started

hooking up with Aunt Bella's PA. Who looks like he's my age? People were posting photos of the two of you all over social media after the Labor Day carnival. It's gross, Mom."

And there it was. "You knew I was seeing someone. I told you at Christmas."

"Why isn't he here?" Devon challenged. "Did you two break up or something?"

"No." My gaze darted away. "He has things to do. With his family. He'd be here if he could."

Devon gave me a long look. "Right."

"It's the truth."

"Okay, then. What about Aunt Bella's baby daddy? Is it the same dude?"

"No, it's not the same dude." If my tone was sharp it was only because Devon was asking the same questions I'd stewed in when I'd first discovered Bella was pregnant. "Their relationship is purely professional."

"So where is he? Why isn't he here helping with this renovation?"

"I told you—"

"Yeah, family stuff." Devon shook his head. "Whatever, Mom."

"Devon Alexandar Allen, don't you dare whatever me," I snapped and snatched the earbud off the end table before he could reinsert it. "I'm your mother and you need to tell me what's going on with you. You're not acting like yourself at all."

His green eyes held a challenge. "I will when you will."

This is why animals eat their young. My lips parted. I didn't know what to say.

"That's what I thought." Devon took the earbud out of my suddenly numb fingers, placed it in his ear, and then rolled on his side, away from me.

I stared at his back for a full minute, trying to gather my thoughts. The mom part of me wanted to pull the do as I say not as I do card. But that was hypocritical as hell. As open as I'd been with Devon, there were things he didn't know.

Like about the Sanders legacy of magic. Like his Aunt Bella had been attacked by members of a rival coven. Axel was staying away not because he wanted to but because he needed to learn how to keep his inner fury under control.

I'd kept my son in the dark for his own good. It looked as though that had suddenly backfired.

Not knowing what else to do, I headed back down to Bella's room. The twins had been fed and bathed and were sleeping peacefully in their cribs. I stared down at them, missing the time when Devon had been that small and it had been my job to protect him from all the crazy in the world and make sure that no matter what, he was fed and had a safe place to sleep.

My heart yearned for the simplicity of those days.

Restless, I wandered the downstairs, from the living room into the unfinished kitchen. My gaze slid to the pantry. Where Axel had first touched me. Being close to him was a kind of reassurance that I hadn't been able to find anywhere else.

"What you want isn't in there, Donna," I muttered to

myself, before making my way out to the conservatory. The scent of night-blooming flowers encouraged me to breathe deeply.

My phone vibrated in my back pocket. I drew it, my heart leaping when I saw the familiar number. "Hey."

"Hey, yourself, Don," Axel murmured in my ear. "How's my girl?"

A thrill went through me. His girl. I was Axel Foley's girl. No matter how hard that was to explain and even at times to believe. "I'm good."

"Liar," he murmured. "I can feel your psychic pain from here."

"Can you?" That was news to me.

"Tippy and Ali are showing me how to connect to familiar mental signatures," he confessed. "Yours was the first one I've tried."

"So, what, you can read my mind now?" I sank onto a metal bench. The cold bit through my jeans. "That seems like yet another unfair fury advantage."

There was a shifting sound, as though he was resettling on the bed. "Not your mind. At least not from this distance. More like your mood."

"And what can you tell from my mood?" I looked up through the glass into the clear night sky and the stars that burned so brilliantly overhead.

"It's been a rough few days," Axel muttered.

I couldn't argue. "Yeah."

"How's Joseline?"

"Better, I think. She's been spending more time with the other wolves."

"So, you've been alone," Axel surmised.

"I've got Bella and the babies to occupy me. Not to mention this endless mess of a renovation."

"So, you've been alone," he said again.

"Devon's here." Not that his visit was a cakewalk. "I think he's suspicious."

"Suspicious of what?"

"All the things I'm suddenly not telling him. I never used to keep things from him."

"It's for his own good, though, right?" Axel prompted.

"That's what I'm telling myself. Only the trouble is I'm not very good at lying, especially to myself."

He chuckled. "I miss you, Don."

"I miss you too." I wanted to ask where he was but knew he wouldn't tell me. "How long are we going to do this?"

He exhaled slowly. "However long it takes for me to control it."

It, as in his inner fury. Male furies were rare and the ones who lived into adulthood went insane, leaving swaths of carnage in their wake. Axel's aunts Tippy and Ali, had taken him away in case the worst happened. And what if it did? Would they even tell me?

"How's that going? Any progress?"

"I'm not sure." It sounded as though he was lying on his back. I pictured him, blond hair disheveled, stretched out with one arm propped beneath his head. "I've been able to tap into our past more. Through lucid dreams."

I sucked in a sharp breath. Our past. He didn't mean this lifetime, but the last one, when he'd been Gunther and I'd been a Healer named Lina who'd died during the witch trials. Gunther had vowed that he would find Lina in the next life and would do whatever it took to keep her safe.

"That's great, isn't it? Did you see what deal Gunther made?"

"Not yet. I can't see anything after that last day, seeing you in the prison."

"Not me," I corrected. "Lina."

"You are Lina though Don," he insisted. "Ali thinks I can't see after that because leaving you and whatever comes next is too traumatic. I'm not ready to see it."

I rose and began pacing. "I'm not sure this is going to work, Axel."

He sucked in an audible breath. "What does that mean?"

"It's just harder than I thought it would be. Not having you here." I'd explained in an earlier phone call about the RSD and how my perception was skewed.

"Are you breaking up with me, Don?"

Was I? That wasn't what I wanted. I wanted him back here, helping me make decisions, reassuring me that I was what he wanted. Not because of who we'd been in a past life but because he wanted me now.

"I don't want that," I breathed and rested my head against the glass. "But I need you here."

"You're killing me, love."

A tear slid down my cheek. "I know. I'm sorry. I wish I was stronger."

"You're plenty strong. You've gone through a total life upheaval in a very short time. You're handling it with grace. The last thing I want is to hurt you," Axel breathed. "That's why I went with them in the first place."

"I know." I swallowed past the lump in my throat. "I guess I'm just feeling sorry for myself. Ignore me."

"Never," he vowed. "I'll never do that, Donna. I think about you every second of every day. I swear to you I'm doing my best to get back to you. You believe me?"

"Yes," I sighed. Through the baby monitor I'd left on the bench I heard the twins stirring. "I should go. Sounds like Ember is waking up."

"Okay." Axel sounded lost. "Night, Don."

"Night." I disconnected and hung my head. Talking to him usually gave me a lift. Helped me look on the bright side and start making plans for his return. This felt like more of a goodbye. The beginning of the end.

What if he never comes back?

More fussing noises crackled through the baby monitor. Taking care of Astrid and Ember might be only a temporary purpose, but it was better than dwelling on what-ifs guaranteed to make me crazy.

I STARED at the red numbers on the alarm clock. 1:45 in the morning. Still no sign of Bella. She'd texted me that she'd gone with the demon back to his hotel and that I should not wait up. What did that mean? Bella was attracted to the demon. Had she decided to sleep with him? It seemed sudden, considering how she hadn't even wanted to call him for a ride the other day.

Ember and Astrid had both had their midnight snack

and had drifted off again. Their steady breaths melded with the quiet shush of the white-noise app on my phone. They'd sleep through until six.

I turned onto my side and stared at the waning moon. The phases of the moon were important to witches. Grand had always claimed the Shadow of Self spell was best done in the dark of the moon, but I didn't want to wait another week to do it.

Decided, I sat up and crept to the armoire where Bella kept her magic supplies. A black pillar candle that smelled of licorice sat inside a ceramic dish. I took it and a lighter over to the mirror alcove, the darkest part of the room. My yellow legal pad sat on the dresser along with a blue Bic pen. I retrieved them both, sat cross-legged on the floor before the mirror, and then lit the wick.

"*Lucerna mea praeteritam aperit.*" Candlelight reveals my past.

It wasn't my own personal past that I was diving into. It was Lina's life I wanted to explore. Axel was doing his part. If I could uncover anything that might help bring him back sooner it was worth a look. I'd been too afraid before, knowing that the witch I'd been before had taken her own life, that Gunther had unwittingly delivered the vial of poison concocted by her sister. He'd put the vial into her hands as she waited in jail for the witch hunters to decide her fate. Lina had gone out on her own terms. The story was sad and tragic. But even though I'd felt the connection, that I'd had flashes from Lina's life, I didn't feel like her.

You are Lina, Axel had said.

Would Axel and I be doomed to the same fate? Not

that there were any modern-day witch hunters to worry about. But were the two of us destined to want what could never be?

Worse, did he only want me because I'd been Lina, the woman he couldn't save? I didn't think I could be with him if that was the case.

My gaze grew fuzzy and unfocused as the candle flame danced in the mirror. My image was nothing but a blurry outline and even that was replaced as the mists of time parted, revealing trees. Not evergreens or maples, but mighty oaks that towered up and blotted out the sun. The ground above their knobby root systems was mossy and plush. Someone sang softly. The words were indistinct, but the melody soothed the anxious knot that had formed in my stomach. It was impossible to tell what time of day it was as the sunlight had to filter through the massive trees, but I got the impression that it was close to dusk. A golden hue backlit a female form crouched by the base of one tree digging up a bit of ground.

The humming stopped and she yanked something free. A plant with vivid purple flowers. I thought it might be echinacea. She placed it in her basket along with the curved-edge knife she'd used to cut the sucker loose. There was nothing familiar about her face. Her hair was strawberry blond, not black as a moonless night. Her eyes were gold-rimmed brown, not the Sander's green that Bella and I had passed on to our offspring. But I recognized something about her. Something that I carried around all day every day.

Lina stared down at her hands and made a face. The

sound of rushing water filled my ears and the image wavered and faded only to be replaced by a different setting. Lina's tattered dress hung over a branch as the woman herself swam beneath a cascade of water that spilled from at least twelve feet above.

My lips parted. The scene looked very much like the enchanted glade that only the magically inclined people could find in the middle of Shadow Cove. Could it possibly be the same spot?

But no, Lina and Gunther had lived in Germany. Still, the waterfall made my heart pound.

The snap of a twig drew Lina's focus behind her. A man stepped out from behind the trees. He was of average height and build with medium brown hair. But his eyes...stormy gray and full of warmth.

Those were Axel's eyes.

He appeared as surprised to see Lina as she was to see him. He spoke, but whatever he said was in German. I snagged the pad, trying to write down the correct words so I could put them through an internet translator later.

Even without understanding what they said though, I could read the energy that passed between them. Lina made a shooing gesture with her hand, and he turned, offering her his back. It was then I spied the blood. His hand was badly mangled, and the bones looked as though they'd been crushed. Once covered, Lina hurried to his side. She reached for him. The second they made contact the vision wavered out of existence.

"What?" I asked when I realized something had blown the candle out. A gust from the vents maybe. The manor was drafty, especially with the renovation still underway. Grabbing my computer off the nightstand I waited impatiently for it to boot up and then tried to type in the words I thought I'd heard.

"I told you not to come back." Lina had said.

Gunther's reply. "I can't stay away."

Lina had lectured him, "It's wrong. You're young enough to be my son."

To which Gunther had answered. "My mother never looked like you."

"Fool," Lina had called him. "I'll have to have sense for us both. Go away."

"You wouldn't refuse to heal an injury." That must have been his hand.

And Lina had ordered him to give her his back.

Bizarre to think that she was me and he was Gunther. That she'd had the same doubts about him, even though it was clear the attraction was mutual.

But as I crawled back into bed, I had to wonder. Would it be worth all the heartache that came after?

CHAPTER 5
BELLA

I should go home. It was on the tip of my tongue to ask Declan to drive me back to Storm Grove after I'd finished my pesto grilled cheese. When he'd offered to take me down into his inner sanctum, the place where he kept his demonic magic, I couldn't refuse. That was why I'd left my children with my twin. Why I'd agreed to our date in the first place.

Not a date. I needed to keep telling myself that no matter how I felt, no matter how scrumptious he looked in his tux, with the jacket draped over a barstool and the tie hanging loose around his neck, looking like a hot guy kicking back after a night on the town.

Without the reek of sulfur wafting off of him, he smelled incredible. He had made my favorite comfort food. And he kept looking at me with that flickering flame of hunger in his gaze. *No, bad Bella. No lusting after the demon.*

With effort, I refocused on the room. It was a converted wine cellar, made entirely of stone. The scent of brimstone clung to the cloth draped over the demon's workbench as well as the paper that hid the trove I desired.

"So, witchling," Declan purred as he watched me survey the scrolls and dusty tomes that lined the floor-to-ceiling shelves. "What exactly are you looking for?"

Power. The word popped into my head. It was a word I'd never coveted before since I'd been born a powerful witch. My innate ability set me apart from most of the magical world and it had made me complacent. I'd taken risks, believing I would find a way out of any trap.

But that had been a false sense of security. I hadn't been strong enough or clever enough when Zeke Bradbury targeted me. I needed the strength to defend myself and my children from anything, including cocksure demons, rogue furies, and other covens that would seek to take from us.

"Protection," I intoned.

Declan tipped his head to the side. "If I might be so bold as to inquire, what is it you want to be protected from?"

"Other witches and warlocks. Demons, wraiths, furies. You know, the usual suspects." Though I strove to keep my voice nonchalant, it quavered a little.

"Witchling, even demon magic can't protect you from every eventuality." Was that pity in his tone?

I rounded to look at him. "Well then what good is it?"

"It's not good, Bella. That's the point. It's power and a corrupt sort of power at that. Believe me when I tell you demonic magic takes much more than it gives."

I turned my back on him. "Now you sound like

Grand. She always said only the desperate dabbled in demon magic."

He sat on a three-legged stool before the workbench and stretched his long legs out before him. "She was wise then. Demonic magic rips away individual choice. It's the bulldozer that takes out anything that stands between the wielder and her goal."

I studied his deliberately casual posture. "Sounds like you don't recommend it."

"To you? I don't." His normally placid face was deadly earnest. "You play with fire when you dabble in demon magic, witchling. Your own kind will turn on you the way they turned on demons. No amount of protection is worth that risk."

Grand's warning had run along a similar track. "I used it before and nothing bad happened. No one detected it. Not even Donna."

Declan shook his head. "Help me to understand why you want this so badly. Why would you risk everything you have here?"

For a moment I wanted to shout at him. To rant and rave that he didn't get what it was like to live in terror. To jump at your own shadow. To go from thinking you were the most badass thing on two legs to being a sad sack mope. But then a sensation I hadn't felt in weeks drew my focus. The pressure, the overfilled sense of a nursing mother whose been separated from her offspring for too long. "Uh oh."

"What's wrong?" The demon stepped closer.

Heat scalded my cheeks. "I need to get home."

"Now? But I thought you were hell-bent to turn into Bessie Badass. What changed?"

I winced as I drew an arm over my breasts. "Don't worry about it. I just need to get home." To where my breast pump sat waiting for me.

Damn it, I'd meant to express enough milk earlier so that this didn't happen. I'd had the thought, but it escaped the same way many of my thoughts did like I was trying to catch mosquitos with a butterfly net. My attention drifted and all those little important tasks that make life possible staged a damn jailbreak, leaving me in a humiliating situation.

The demon's gaze dropped to my chest and his midnight eyes grew heavy-lidded. "Oh, I *see*."

"Quit staring," I snapped as I tried to rearrange my shawl to hide the damp fabric. I could feel the moisture seeping through the bodice of the purple dress. Damn it, I knew I should have worn a different dress, one that would conceal a nursing bra and some of those pad things to absorb any mild spillage.

"It's nothing to be embarrassed about, witchling. I've seen you nursing the twins."

"So will you take me home now?" Never again. Never again would I allow the demon to drive me anywhere. If I had to deal with him in the future, I'd meet him somewhere and drive off even if I had to take Donna's ugly little sedan.

"Not just yet," he murmured. "How about a trade?"

Did he want to make a bargain *now?* "I haven't even collected on the last deal. What the hell could you possibly want so badly...?"

His gaze riveted on my chest and flames flared higher.

I scurried away until my back hit the wall. "No. Do you hear me? *No*. Nothing is worth that."

"Not even an open-ended favor of your choosing?" Declan hadn't moved. At least he wasn't crowding me, pressuring me with anything but his words. "We both know you're growing addicted to demonic magic. You're going to want more from me."

The silky-smooth way he said those words...My teeth sank into my lower lip. What he was offering... an open-ended favor without a limit or definition. That was what had lost me the deed to Storm Grove. I could get it back. If I let him do what he wanted, I could demand the manor back. After he finished the renovations. Donna would be thrilled.

But what he wanted. To let him suckle milk from my breasts that way. I shook my head. "I'm not a sex worker here to see to your fetishes, demon."

"No, you're a woman in need. Tell me why it's so wrong for me to help you rather than the inanimate piece of plastic that'll do the exact same thing?"

He'd struck a nerve. I loathed the breast pump. The sound, the suction. I used it so others could feed the twins and would have to use it again until all the alcohol was out of my system. In a weird way what he said made sense.

"Just that?" I whispered.

What are you doing? My inner sense of self sounded a lot like my sister when Donna got up on her high horse. *You aren't considering letting him touch you!*

Maybe.... My nipples had grown stiff, and the wet fabric of the dress clung to my breasts obscenely. Relief was within reach. That and the deed to the house. Would it be so bad if I wanted it?

Wanted him?

The corner of his lips curled up. "Of course. You don't think I'd take shameless advantage of you, do you witchling?"

"Yes," I snapped, and he grinned a wicked grin.

He offered me his hand, waiting for the shake and the words that would seal the pact. "Come here."

I could run. Kick off my heels and head for the stairs. Through the lobby where the night clerk and anyone loitering there would see my problem. More people whispering about me didn't bother me. I had a reputation around Shadow Cove. I could hold my head high and, soggy garment and all, I would sail out of the hotel like a ship under full sail.

But my shoes stayed on as I took one step, then another, and another until I stood before him. My knees shook but I lifted my chin. "A bargain then."

Surprise flashed in his dark eyes. He hid it quickly, but I'd seen it. He hadn't thought I'd go for it. An odd sense of pride fluttered in my chest. Not much surprised Declan. His hand was warm as he slid his palm against mine. "A bargain well struck."

I swallowed and gripped his hand. It was warm and smooth and engulfed mine.

The metallic zing of magic filled the space between our bodies as the bargain was sealed. "Turn around."

Could he hear my heart thundering in my chest?

Worse, did he see the slight tremor in my legs, the wobble as I slowly pivoted and presented my back?

His hands didn't touch my bare flesh. Not like when we'd been dancing. Still, I could feel his aura brush over mine as though he was moving his hands a hairsbreadth along my spine, following the gentle line to the nape of my neck. I swallowed and tucked my chin, exposing the knot that held my dress up.

He tugged lightly, once, twice, and then the straps slithered down past my shoulders. The cling of wet material dared defy gravity, the milk all that stood between my bare breasts and the demon's blazing gaze.

Instead of ordering me to turn again, Declan urged me to pivot. My breaths came in small, nervous pants as I completed the full circle and stopped before him. Perched on the stool his face was on par with my breasts. I'd expected his attention to be focused there. After all, that was what he wanted, for whatever reason. Instead, those burning eyes were on my face. He studied me for a long moment. What was he looking for? Reassurance? Some telltale sign that I would panic and bolt?

His hands stayed in his lap. He didn't reach for me, didn't fall on me like a ravaging beast. I appreciated that and managed to steady my breathing. The dress shifted a little and through sheer force of will I managed to keep my hands from flying up to hold the garment in place. Finally, after what felt like an eternity, those dark eyes traveled down my bare neck and traced lightly over my collarbones and shoulders before he reached out with his hands, snagging the ends of my forgotten shawl. He pulled, drawing the fabric tight and I felt pressure on my lower back, urging me to take a step forward. To come even closer to him.

I did. A sheet of paper wouldn't have fit between him and my breasts. I expected him to drop the ends of the shawl and peel the clinging material down. He did neither. Still holding me tight to him, he leaned forward on the stool ever so slightly and nuzzled my left breast.

A groan escaped along with more milk. My body's intelligence knew to let down for a rooting babe. The motion was deliberate, and he nuzzled deeper. His hot breaths made me shiver, the throb in my full breasts growing unbearable. He pulled back long enough to look into my eyes before his tongue emerged.

His pointed tongue.

He swiped at my nipple, clearly visible beneath the sodden fabric. A strangled sound escaped as he did it again, and again. Wicked, decadent demon.

The force of his nuzzling separated the fabric from my skin. He clamped his teeth on the edge of the dress and drew it down. I shivered as the cool air brushed over my damp skin.

His hot mouth was there. Sucking on my nipple, swallowing the milk he brought forth. One hand released the hold on my shawl to cup the other breast, which throbbed in time with his greedy pulls.

My hands flew up and tunneled through his hair. My legs shook now, not from fear but from need. Oh, *so* much better than the breast pump.

He made a gruff sound, what might have been a groan and then released my nipple. I expected him to switch to the other side, but something in his frantic manner eased. Instead that pointed tongue appeared once more and swiped along the underside of my breasts. As though he wanted to consume every last drop.

"Please," I whispered as the pressure on the other side grew until I felt sure I would burst. He didn't speak. There were no taunts, no sly comments. He knew what I wanted, and with unerring accuracy, held my gaze even as he took my right nipple into his mouth.

Instant relief. My head tipped back and I stared up at the ceiling, wanting to sigh, to weep at how good it felt. Better than good. There was something there beneath the ease that came from expressing milk. It was dark, hot, and coiled down low in my belly. The draws grew languid, and I felt an answering throb between my legs with every pull.

This was way more than I'd bargained for. Arousal burned hotter, a fire that had almost gone out completely now sparked back to life. I glanced down, lost because Declan's gaze was still on my face, eyes drinking in my expression the way his lips did my milk.

This was wrong. Dangerous. I wanted to beg him to stop. But if I did before he finished would that nullify our bargain?

That wasn't why I held my tongue though. I didn't want him to stop. I wanted him to keep going. To peel the dress the rest of the way down and touch me between my legs. I wanted to keep feeling these hot, exciting feelings that I'd all but forgotten about. The pleasure.

Stars above, he made my blood pump, my adrenaline spike, and got all my juices flowing.

Declan was the ultimate dopamine rush.

I was on the verge of begging him to touch me more when he drew away. I blinked, still lost in the pleasure of his mouth, the sensations that had been buried for over a year.

"I think that's enough," he said.

"What?" I shook my head, dazed by lust and foggy with confusion.

He didn't reply. Instead, he got up and moved to my back. He swept the loose tendrils of hair out of the way with a light brush and then reached around to pull up my top. He tied a quick knot and then murmured, "I'll have someone take you home."

Someone. He wasn't going to drive me? After what we had just been doing?

Shame assailed me from all sides. What had I expected? He hadn't kissed me, hadn't made any promises outside the bargain. So what right did I have to expect anything other than a dismissal?

Why did what had felt incredible and empowering only seconds before now fill me with self-loathing?

Without a word, I lifted my chin, wrapped my shawl around my still-tingling breasts, and stalked up the stairs.

It was only when I was settled in the back of a town car that I realized I'd left without the protection spell I'd wanted.

CHAPTER 6
DONNA

The sound of a car pulling away had dragged me from sleep a little after three. Before I could turn on the light, the bedroom door opened, and my twin crawled into bed beside me. When I asked how her date was, she murmured a terse, fine, and then rolled over and went to sleep.

I'd slipped back upstairs and gone to my own room. Joseline was spending the night at the bunkhouse, so I'd stared out the window and wondered what had happened between my sister and the demon.

By the time I headed down for my first cup of the magic bean juice that made all things possible, she'd risen with the twins and had them strapped into highchairs in the conservatory. Astrid and Ember were transitioning to eating strained pears and oatmeal along with Zwieback biscuits to help with teething. All these things made a colossal mess and I'd put drop cloths down beneath the highchairs since this was our main hub of operations.

For convenience's sake, we'd moved the coffee pot along with the crock pot and enough dishes for the four of us to a sideboard. I'd originally planned to go into town for doughnuts, craving a lift after last night. But Bella didn't even look my way when I suggested it.

"Axel called last night," I began as I sat down with my coffee on a bench.

"Mhhmm," Bella kept her gaze on Ember who was smearing his cereal in his baby fine tufts.

"He's working on lucid dreaming and past life regression," I continued.

"That's good," Bella made an exaggerated happy face and then pretended to eat a spoonful of Astrid's breakfast. The little girl twisted around in her seat as far as she could go, refusing to be duped.

"And Devon's dropped out of school so he can run away with the circus," I added in a bland voice. "He wants to be the bearded lady."

"Good, good," Bella made yummy sounds for an instant and then scowled at me. "What?"

I laughed at her. "I knew you weren't listening."

"Sorry," she said. "My mind's on other things."

"Like Declan?" I asked in my most innocent tone.

"Do not mention that demon's name to me again," she barked.

I blinked. "Whoa. Okay. What the hell, Bella? We can't not mention him when he owns the house. I need to work with him to get the place up and running."

"There won't be a B&B," she insisted. "I'm going to get Storm Grove back. It's as good as done."

That was something. "Great. How?"

"Never mind how." She wilted a little but then I saw her spine straighten and her chin lift. "So, you have no idea why Devon's here and not at school?"

"Maybe an idea," I murmured. "He's upset about Axel, and he thinks I'm keeping things from him."

"You are," Bella pointed out.

"I don't have a choice." Devon was a dud, a non-magical child of a magical parent. Because until recently I'd believed I was a dud too, I'd kept the truth of our witchy lineage from my son. From personal experience, I knew how lousy it felt to believe you were swimming in the shallow end of your gene pool.

"It's too much," I groaned. "And too late. If I tell him everything now it will overwhelm him."

"What if he's like you, though?" Bella said. "A late bloomer. Wouldn't it be better for him to know his heritage before magic railroads him?"

She had a point. Draining my coffee mug, I decided I'd ruminate on it while I went over the day's punch list. "The contractors will be here by ten. What are you doing today?"

"I thought I'd take the twins down to the bunkhouse and then maybe for a walk. If it doesn't rain." She made a face as she peered through the glass at the dark sky.

"Okay. Just keep your cell on you in case I need to reach you." Not that I would. Bella had been no help with the renovations. I tried not to take it personally because she was occupied with the twins. One look at the dark circles under her green eyes though and I reached out and put a hand on her shoulder. "Was it that bad?"

She jumped. "What do you mean?"

"Whatever it was he who shall not be named had you do last night?"

"Oh." She blinked as though she'd forgotten all about it. "Yeah, it was a little upsetting. I don't know why. Using my gift that way has never bothered me before."

"It'll be all right." I gave her shoulder one more easy squeeze and then headed upstairs. So, my sister did have a line when it came to using her gift. And crossing that line had surprised her. In the past, she'd always been able to justify using her reflection to hoodwink people, especially people she needed something from. Skirting a parking ticket or getting a better deal on her internet package. We weren't white witches and often utilized magic for personal gain. But whatever the demon had Bella do somehow crossed into the gray area where she'd never gone before. Instinct told me utilizing her power for Declan's benefit was only part of what was bothering her though.

Had something happened with the demon? I knew he had designs on her. It had been clear from the first moment I'd seen them together. Sexual tension crackled between the pair of them. Bella had been fighting hard to ignore it. Maybe because of the situation—she was the witch who'd summoned him—or perhaps because of her past trauma. I didn't know and much like the situation with Devon, there wasn't a damn thing I could do about it until the other party decided to confide.

It was too cold for a shower, and I didn't want to risk having the power, or worse the water, cut out when I was in the middle of my ablution. I dressed in jeans and threw a flannel over a form-fitting tank top. After twisting my hair up in a messy ponytail, I collected my phone and computer chargers, intending to set up shop in the conservatory for the morning.

Outside Devon's door, I paused. I didn't like how the conversation had gone the night before. And while in my heart of hearts, I still didn't think my son could handle the magical reveal and all it entailed, I needed to try again to get through to him. He'd mentioned that I hadn't been to any of his soccer games. Was that the source of his discontent?

"Devon?" I called as I rapped lightly on the door. "You awake? I was going to get doughnuts—"

A scurrying sound, like something scrambling, made me pause mid-sentence. "Devon?"

"Get out!" I heard my son shout. He didn't sound angry as much as terrified. I didn't think he was addressing me.

I tried the handle. Locked. Dropping the cords, I pounded on the door, every instinct I possessed on full alert. "Devon, open up!"

"Donna?" Bella called from the foot of the stairs. "What's going on?"

A scream carried through the door, followed by a thud.

"Get the skeleton key," I bellowed. The locks on all the bedroom doors were the old-fashioned kind where the key remained inside the lock. There was a master skeleton key that would open any door in the house though.

"Where is it?" Bella called.

Shit shit shit. Where had I used it last? Where would I

have put it so that either of us could find it if the need arose?

"Try your bedroom. The jewelry box," I yelled.

There was no sound coming from the bedroom. The silence scared the hell out of me. "Devon!" I screamed and pummeled the door with both fists. "Open this door!"

No response. Damn it, what was happening in there? I should have known better than to let him stay at the manor. Things happened at Storm Grove. Things like wraiths and werewolves, demons, and rival covens attacking. Guilt warred with fear in the pit of my belly. "Bella?"

"I found it!" My sister ran up the stairs, hiking up her long skirts so she could ascend two at a time. I ran to her and snatched the key out of her grip. I headed for the locked door, my hand shaking as I jabbed the skeleton key in from the far side then wrenched the handle to the right, shoving the door with all my adrenaline-fueled strength.

At first, I thought the key hadn't worked. The handle turned but the door didn't budge. "Help me," I begged my sister.

Together the two of us pushed and shoved our way into the room. I had to strangle a scream when I realized the thing that had been blocking the door was my son's body. Devon lay prone, his face turned away from us.

"Devon." I fell to my knees beside him and reached for his neck, desperate to find a pulse. I didn't breathe until the carotid artery throbbed under my touch. "He's alive."

Bella had pulled magic into her hands and was scouring the room. "Did something attack him? I see blood even though the room is clear."

I glanced up to see where she was pointing at the sheet. Dark red smudges stained the snowy fabric.

"Devon," I called, afraid to touch him more or turn him over. What if he had a head injury? Or maybe it was his spine? "Bella, call the Healer."

"On it." My sister hopped over my legs and headed down the stairs to retrieve her cell.

"Talk to me, Devon," I begged.

His eyes opened. I drew back with a cry. It was cut off as he lunged for me, his eyes crazed. I gasped in shock as his hands went around my neck. Bloody rivulets had been carved in his face, four long craggy stripes. His green eyes were those of a stranger as he squeezed my throat, choking me.

I tried scrambling away, but he was too strong. He'd cut off my air, I couldn't speak, couldn't plead with him not to do this. He'd regret it. I refused to let him kill me. The guilt of that alone would destroy him. My hands clawed at the floor, hunting for something, *anything*, that I could use to fend him off. There was nothing though. No handy crowbar or broom or bat.

My vision was fading around the edges. My lungs burned. *Air*, my wonky brain pleaded.

A crash sounded and glass exploded around us. The flash of light, the swoop of wings. Devon's crazed eyes rolled up in his head and he collapsed on top of me.

"What. The. Shit?" I wheezed as a familiar set of male

63

hands rolled my son's limp form off me. I looked up into lightning-streaked gray irises.

"Are you okay?" Axel asked. The wings folded back and there was a flash as he shifted from his fury form back to the familiar human one.

My throat burned like I'd been chowing down on hot coals, but I nodded. He helped me sit up and once I was sure I wouldn't keel over, I crawled back to Devon's side. He was out this time, fully unconscious.

When I glanced up at Axel, he read the question in my eyes.

"I was coming back. After that call last night, I was worried about you. I was just a few miles out when your fear swamped my mental grid. Who is this?" He glanced down at my son's inert form.

"Devon," I rasped. "What did you do to him?"

He held up a jar. "It's the potion I've been taking to help me lucid dream. After I broke the window and he didn't respond, I dosed him so I could get you free I'm glad I didn't listen to my instinct to kill him."

So was I. "There's something wrong with him." I held up his right hand and showed Axel the blood and skin beneath the nails. "He did that to himself."

"Healer is on the way," Bella's voice cut off in the hall as she took in the scene. The broken window, an unconscious Devon several feet from where she'd left him, Axel standing there in ripped jeans and a wrinkled T-shirt. Me, panting and struggling to right my breathing. She took in the scene and then turned to me for an explanation.

"He tried to kill me." I pointed at Devon, so she knew which he I meant.

Bella scowled and then looked to Axel who simply said, "I was in the neighborhood."

I reached out and squeezed his arm. "Good thing too."

"Save your voice, Don. The Healer might need you to answer questions." He studied Devon and then murmured, "We should restrain him in case he wakes up and tries to hurt anyone else, himself included."

Though Declan was a solidly built five foot eleven inches, Axel had no problem picking him up and arranging him on the bed. I found some old drapery cords that he used with sheets to bind Devon to the mattress while Bella fetched a broom and dustpan to clean up the glass.

"What's wrong with him?" I asked as I swept. Bella's arms were around herself, but I didn't think it had anything to do with the winter wind that gusted through the uncovered window. "Have you ever seen something like this before?"

"In wraiths," she said. "But we haven't had any of those since we sealed the demon portal. I'll go check the mirror."

I swallowed and then grimaced at the discomfort. With Devon secure Axel moved to examine my throat. His hands shook as he reached for my face. "Stars above, Don. You've got a burst blood vessel in your eye. He was seconds away from killing you. If I hadn't already been on my way back here...." A shudder shook his big body.

I reached up and touched his face and mouthed the words, "I'm okay."

"I'll go get something for the swelling," he said. "And a piece of plywood to cover that window."

"Later," I whispered. I clung to him, not wanting him out of my sight. After a moment he gave up, clearly unwilling to be separated from me either.

Bella reappeared, her gaze troubled. "Not a wraith."

We all turned to face the bed.

What the hell had happened to my son?

CHAPTER 7
BELLA

Matilda Longshanks had been to Storm Grove more times than any other witch outside of the Sanders family. The local Healer had helped deliver my children and she occasionally sat for them when Donna and I both needed to go somewhere. She arrived a few minutes after picking up my call. I met her at the door. She smelled of dried lavender and thyme and her red curls were constantly disheveled.

"Where's the patient?" she asked, her New England accent brisk and to the point as always.

"Upstairs." I took her cloak and hat and hung them on the coatrack Donna had unearthed from the stars alone knew where. That was my sister, forever discovering old junk and putting it to good use.

Matilda hiked up her skirts and made for the stairs at a speed I wouldn't have thought she was capable of. I had no idea of her age and had never been bold enough to ask, though I knew she had treated our Grand for chickenpox when she'd been a child.

I followed her pumpkin-shaped backside up and hovered in the doorway. Axel and Donna were still in the room, on the far side of the bed.

"Go check on the babes." It took me a moment to realize the Healer was speaking to me.

"Oh, of course." Had I really forgotten them? Hurrying downstairs, I made for the conservatory at breakneck speed. Donna and I had set up a play area in the space, with a large blue mat that the twins could roll around on and an octagonal playpen that kept them contained. Still, that was no excuse for leaving them unattended. Images of all the things that might have gone wrong marched through my mind. They could have choked on a small object, or someone could have come in through the back door and taken one of them. My heart pounded and my palms were coated in sweat as I rounded the last turn and stopped dead.

Worse than I even imagined.

The demon was seated in the large play area, Astrid on his knee. He made faces at my daughter, even as his free hand rubbed Ember's pudgy belly, making the little boy laugh. Mixed emotions coursed through me. Of course, Declan was in the habit of showing up at the manor whenever he wanted. And he often held the twins or played with them. I always thought it was his way of getting under my skin. But seeing him like this, in such an unguarded moment, a lump formed in my throat.

After his curt dismissal the night before I thought he'd stay away. I needed him to stay away so I could forget what happened.

Ember rolled from his back onto his side and from

there up onto all fours. He crawled closer to Declan, and I watched in awe as he gripped hold of the demon's free arm and pulled himself upright. His sturdy little legs trembled but he was standing on his own two feet.

My hand flew to my mouth and tears stung my eyes as I witnessed the milestone. Astrid could already hold herself up and even took steps while walking along the furniture. But Ember had been determined to crawl everywhere.

"That a lad," Declan murmured in his silky, midnight croon. Did he have any idea that was the first time Ember had stood on his own? And the intention behind the move had been my son's driving desire to get closer to the demon who was grinning down at him with an expression of utter pride.

That look tore my heart in half. I must have made some sort of noise because Declan looked up and caught me standing in the doorway.

"Ah, there you are, witchling." His tone was breezy. As if the night before hadn't happened.

"This isn't a good time," I told him as I stepped over the low fence into the play area and picked Ember up. His dimpled fists curled immediately around my hair but to my irritation, he turned his head so he could keep staring at the demon. "We've got some sort of situation."

"Ah, you know about it then." Declan shifted his grip on Astrid and rose to his full height, so he was once again looking down at me.

I frowned. "Know about what?"

"The mortals have all gone...what is that graphic human expression? Apeshit."

"I don't understand." I let out a tight squeak as Ember tugged just a little too hard on my hair.

"My employees and the guests at the hotel are hallucinating. Badly. Some turned violent. I need you and your sister to conjure a sleeping spell to knock them out until I can locate the source of the contaminant."

That sounded like exactly what had happened with Devon. "You need to go tell Donna and Axel about this. Donna's son was affected too."

Declan's dark brows pulled down. "Here as well? That's not a good sign, witchling. Here." He shifted Astrid to my other hip and once the little girl was secure, vanished from sight.

I let out a nervous breath. I wanted to know what was happening in the room at the top of the hall. But Declan had mentioned contamination. The last thing I wanted was to expose Ember or Astrid to whatever had infected their cousin.

Instead, I set my son and daughter down and tried to encourage Ember to stand again, even going as far as putting him on his sock-clad feet and holding him upright. He fell back onto his diapered bottom with a laugh.

"Okay, fine. I get the message. You'll stand in your own time." I kissed the top of his head and breathed him in, glad that for the moment my son was hale and healthy.

Poor Donna. I couldn't even get my head around the fact that Axel had reappeared. Was he fixed? Somehow, I doubted it. But I couldn't order him to leave, not when he'd saved my sister's life.

Restless, I set the children down and then turned on the small television that Donna had secured to the wall. We'd grown up without television and I never would have considered installing one, but Donna had insisted certain programs helped "get her mind off things". This was the first I'd ever touched the device. I flipped through channels, hunting for some sort of distraction. The headline on the bottom of the screen caught my eye. *Town gripped by hallucinations.*

The image on the screen was a familiar one. A white wooden sign with black lettering read, *Welcome to Shadow Cove, a hidden gem worth discovering.* Besides the town sign a woman in a red scarf and a black peacoat spoke clearly into a microphone. "I'm standing here at the town line to Shadow Cove, a quaint mountain community. As of this morning, 911 dispatch has picked up over two dozen calls from everything raging from fires that don't exist to attacks by friends and families. Sources say residents seem to be experiencing some sort of mass hallucination. No word yet on what's affected this normally sleepy community."

I thought of what Declan had said about the guests and staff at his hotel, who'd been perfectly fine the night before, suddenly acting out of character. I thought about Devon's attack on Donna. One thought stuck in my head.

I smell magic.

"Could it be an attack?" Donna asked as she paced the bedroom floor. To keep the contractors away from my magical stores I'd moved all of my witchy bits and bobs into my bedroom. It made for tight crafting quarters, even tighter with my sister so spun up. "Something from another coven?"

"Keep your voice down," I told her as I stirred the sleeping draft the demon had requested. "We don't want Matilda to think we're talking about her coven."

Donna ran a hand through her snarled hair. "That's not what I meant. I was talking about the Bradburys."

"They're gone," I said shortly and stirred with more vigor. "All of them. They can't hurt us anymore."

I was supposed to stir the concoction one hundred counterclockwise strokes before Donna, and I spoke the incantation. It was as good an idea as any, putting the hallucinating folks into a magically induced coma until we figured out what was causing the hallucinations. Much like the fairies in the tale of Sleeping Beauty, my sister and I could enchant our little corner of the globe to sleep and miss out on the action. Though with reporters lurking at the town line, someone would pick up on the change soon enough. We didn't have much time to figure out what was causing the hallucinations.

Donna put her hand on my shoulder. "I'm sorry. I didn't mean to bring up bad memories."

"You have just as many as I do." I made the sixty-seventh stir and then added, "And no, I don't think a rival witch coven would do this. As far as we know, none of the magical people have been affected. Just regular humans and duds. Why would a coven go after them?"

Donna resumed her pacing. "I don't know what to think, what to do."

"Breathe, Donna." I knew she was scared, knew she wanted nothing more than to race up the stairs and stand by Devon's bedside. Matilda hadn't had any luck. "There's nothing to Heal," The witch had murmured. "Not beyond his face. There's no mental injury my magic can perceive."

So, the sleeping draft was our best bet until we discovered the source of the contamination.

"Contamination," I muttered as I made the eighty-eighth stroke. "That's what the demon said."

"What?" Donna scowled at me. "Why does that matter?"

Because somehow Declan knew that whatever was wrong wasn't a virus or something with a natural cause. He knew something he hadn't shared with us. I needed to find out what.

But one thing at a time. My sister wasn't in the mood to speculate, and I didn't want to heap stress onto her plate.

I performed the final stroke and then beckoned her forward. "Ready with the spell?"

"You sure we don't need to do this one in Latin?" Donna asked.

"It's all about intention. Latin puts us in the frame of mind to work magic, but I don't doubt either of our intentions is focused on making sure no one else gets hurt."

Donna nodded and together the two of us held hands. A phantom wind swirled through the room, the spirit plane responding to our unity even before we spoke the first syllable.

"Give surcease to the innocent, let them rest and dream not. Mortal and dud, your time has come. From this moment until we deem it safe to wake. Sleep. Sleep. Sleep."

As the final word rang through the room, the liquid in the cauldron bubbled higher until a purple fog lifted from the rim. The ethereal wind sucked the fog up, creating a purple vortex. The entire potion boiled off into a gas that the spirit wind claimed.

Donna let go of my hand and headed for the door even as I darted for the window. The wind split and carried the magic fog out through the window, the open door, and even up the chimney. I stood still for a moment and watched the purple cloud head down the mountainside toward the heart of Shadow Cove. Ironic that the townspeople had feared me for years, afraid that I would hex them. And now I was, or rather we were, but only to save them from themselves.

Donna headed back upstairs to check on her son. Since Matilda had agreed to stay with the children, I hunted for the demon.

I found him on the front porch, watching the purple fog settle over the town. "How did you know there was contamination? I asked him. "Have you seen this before?"

"Not on this scale," Declan said slowly. "But yes. This sort of madness stems from the demonic plane. There must have been a rupture somewhere. A rift that's oozing out into this world and allowing all the hate and fear that dwells there to escape and affect the mortals."

"Why just them?" I asked. "Why aren't we affected?"

"Magical folks have layers of protection. Mental

shields and spirit guides offer us shields against mystical attacks. But they won't last forever. Eventually, we too will succumb."

I swallowed. And there would be no one left to save us.

"Do you know what caused the rupture?"

The demon turned to look at me and I thought I saw a flash of pity in his eyes as he murmured "I believe you did, witchling."

CHAPTER 8
DONNA

"How long can you stay?" I whispered to Axel as I shut the bedroom door. Whispering was unnecessary. Between Axel's powder and the sleep charm Bella and I had worked, there wasn't much chance Devon would wake up. Still, it felt like when I'd put my son down for a nap as a toddler and my wonky brain reverted to hushed tones.

Axel shifted his weight. "Not long. I should leave before sundown."

Sundown. My teeth sank into my lower lip. I needed him here, helping me figure this thing out. But it wasn't fair to put my stress on him. So, I just nodded.

"Don," He reached for me. I went willingly into his arms and let him hold me close. The steady thud of his heartbeat helped me draw in a shaky breath. Followed by another and another. He smelled of ozone and spring rain. I wished I could bottle his scent and take a hit anytime I needed reassurance.

"I don't want to leave you like this. Dealing with all of this," he murmured into my hair.

"You don't have a choice." Though it felt like my heart was being ripped from my chest, I gave him one last squeeze and took a step back. "I know you need to leave. I can handle things here."

Maybe.

His gaze swept over my face. "I know you can. You're the most capable person I've ever met."

"You must not get out much," I quipped.

"Don't do that." Axel scowled.

"Do what?"

"Put yourself down like that. You're insulting the woman I love and admire. And every time you do you're casting a spell over yourself."

My lips parted. The words had come out automatically. A joke to diffuse the tension. And I was always the butt of it. Axel was right. I did cast a spell of doubt over myself. Life was hard enough without being my own bully. "It's a bad habit. I'll try and break it."

"Good." Reaching for my hand, he drew me toward the curved stairs. "Now, let's go see what Bella and Declan found out. If there's anything I can do to help before I must go, I need to get on it."

We headed down the stairs and while Axel have gone on to the conservatory, I paused in the front hall, my gaze going to the inscription in the lintel. "I think we should wake Bonnie and Clyde. There are no humans around to spot them and if someone is trying to attack us, they'll be at the ready."

Axel squeezed my hand. "See what I mean? Capable."

I smiled at him, lifted my chin, and threw my shoulders back before speaking the words that would wake the gargoyles perched outside. A moment later a large fist pounded on the door. I opened it and stared up and up into the grinning stone face of Clyde.

"Good morrow, Dove." The gargoyle tipped an imaginary hat to me. The sight of him and the sound of his Cockney accent made me smile. There was a time when I thought I'd never hear his voice again, but Axel had done what he did best—fixed what was broken.

Clyde, me. It didn't matter. The man was an unstoppable force of nature.

"What's the word?" Bonnie asked.

I brought them up to speed about the contamination ending with, "If you two are willing, I'd like you to keep an eye on the town. Make sure the sleep charm holds and that no one is wandering around creating mayhem."

"No worries, Dove. We've got your back." Clyde ducked his huge stone head again and then the pair took off, heading toward the fog-shrouded town.

"That's done," I said to Axel. "Now we need to find Bella and her demon and come up with a game plan."

"Her demon?" Axel raised a blond brow. "Did I miss something?"

I shrugged. "Nothing official. They went on a date last night and Bella was out all hours. She was in a foul mood this morning so either things went very well and she's in a tailspin, or they tanked completely."

"Well, I know what I'm hoping for." Axel threaded

his fingers with mine and then raised my knuckles to his lips. "And not just because I plan to ask him for money."

"You like him," I said with sudden realization.

"Don't you?"

I thought about it for a beat. "I do. Everything I was ever taught told me that demons are foul horrible creatures, that they were responsible for wraiths descending on mankind, and that their magic was the darkest sort. But Declan isn't like that. He's ruthless when it comes to business. But the way he is with Bella...he's good for her."

"Whatever you do, don't tell her that," Axel winked. "Act like you hate the idea of them together. She'll be even more drawn to him if he's forbidden."

"Yeah, kinda like it worked for us?" I winked so he knew I was teasing.

He paused and then turned, crowding in on me until my back hit the wall. "It doesn't matter what anyone else said or did. My heart belongs to you."

I wrapped my arms around his neck and stood on my tiptoes. "Kiss me," I breathed.

Axel pulled me tight against him. His lips were soft as they brushed lightly over my own. Once, twice, and once more. He made to pull away, but my fingers tunneled into his hair. Burying themselves in the thick blond mass. It had grown longer in the six months since I'd seen him last. More like Gunther's. The thought broke the lust spell that had settled over us.

"I had this dream about you the other night," Axel whispered.

"Me or Lina?" I teased.

"I keep telling you, you are Lina."

"What was I doing in this dream?"

"Being stubborn."

My jaw dropped. "I'm not stubborn,"

He smirked. "Yeah, right. I injured my hand. I think maybe I'd done it on purpose, so I had a reason to go see you again."

My lips parted. That was the same memory I'd witnessed with the Shadow of Self spell.

"It's funny. But while I was having that dream, I could have sworn you were with me. I could even smell you," he murmured nuzzling my neck.

"If you two are finished," the demon crooned from the doorway. "We have an interdimensional rift to locate."

"So let me get this straight." I held out my hands as I looked from Declan to my twin and then down to the map they'd spread out. Shadow Cove had been circled with a large red line. "You're saying there's a rift between the demon world and ours and that's what's causing everyone to go nuts?"

"In theory," Declan folded his arms behind his back.

"Why didn't we have this problem with the portal?" I asked.

"Portals, like the one you sealed off, were designed as drawbridges. They can only be lowered from this side.

Much like demons need to be summoned inside a circle, everything about the demonic plane is designed so nothing can escape. The rift is different because it started in the demonic realm and broke through to our side. The transit isn't safe to venture, but that doesn't keep things from seeping out."

"Any ideas what caused the rift?" Axel asked.

Good question. I glanced at the demon, waiting for an explanation.

Declan looked back down at the map. "Only theories. What matters now is finding the rift and sealing it shut."

"And that will make everyone better?" My teeth sank into my lower lip. Axel put an arm around my shoulders.

The demon lifted his dark gaze to hold mine. "Unfortunately, I have no idea. This has never happened before."

I sagged. Axel wrapped an arm around my shoulders, an easy gesture of support.

"But it's the best place to start," Bella piped up. "You said so."

She sounded almost as desperate as I felt. I shot her an appreciative smile, glad she was in my corner.

"True," Declan's tone was grim. "But we're going to have to locate the rift and then seal it. It won't be easy."

My hands clenched into fists at my sides. "I'll do whatever it takes."

"Me too," Bella nodded.

Declan and Axel exchanged a look. "You'll escort them?" Axel asked.

"I will." The demon nodded.

I glanced out the glass windows that overlooked the western sky. The sun was halfway down it. Only a few precious hours left until sunset.

"Axel," Bella asked. "May I speak with you a moment?"

"Sure, Bells." The two of them moved off to the side, leaving me with the demon.

"Be sure you know what you're doing, Donna Sanders-Allen," Declan urged. "Even once we locate the rift we need to find a way to seal it closed. And using magic around portals can be treacherous."

"Whatever it takes," I said, even as images of the fall I'd taken into the demon underworld flashed through my mind.

"You say that now," Declan murmured, "But there's no way to prepare for what will happen.

"What's it like?" I asked him. "The demonic realm?"

His gaze went unfocused. "There's no way to describe the misery of it. The cold that freezes the marrow or the heat that threatened the seer the flesh from one's bones until they threaten to break."

I gave him a level look. "I'm perimenopausal and my son is in danger. No hell realm will stop me."

He held up both hands. "Whatever you say."

Axel moved back to my side and the demon strode off to join Bella. "I'm going to fly over the town and see if I can spot the rift from the air. Want to come with me?"

I did, but I shook my head. "I need to prepare for this trip. What did Bella want?"

He glanced over his shoulder. "She asked me to take the twins with me when I leave."

My lips parted. "You're serious?"

"Shocked me too. But she wants them safely away from here. Besides, Matilda Longshanks has already agreed to watch over Devon. She can't do that and take care of Astrid and Ember." His throat bobbed. "It's nice to know she's beginning to trust me again."

"You're a good guy, Axel Foley." I squeezed his arm. "Go now. I'll see you before sunset."

He nodded and then headed for the door.

Declan touched Bella's shoulder. "I need to collect a few things from my inner sanctum."

She flinched, though I didn't think it was from his touch. "Be back by sunset."

He bobbed his head and then vanished.

"I need to pack," Bella murmured, turning toward her room. "Will you watch the twins until Axel gets back?"

"Of course."

She was halfway to the door when I called out, "Hey, Bella?"

She glanced at me over her shoulder.

"It means a lot to him that you're trusting Axel with the twins. A lot to both of us."

Her smile was sad. "I just want them to be safe. And right now, the more immediate threat is the rift, not the fury who might one day go ballistic."

"Still," I said. "Thank you."

Her green gaze turned haunted as she murmured, "Don't thank me, Donna. Please."

"Your mom is stressed," I told Astrid as I sat beside her in the playpen. "Not that I blame her."

The little girl had been crawling around as though hunting for an exit. As though she wanted to be part of the adult conversation. Ember had fallen asleep, his thumb inserted into his mouth. Twins just like Bella and me, each was a unique creature.

I played patty-cake with Astrid and then sang the five little ducks song, counting down until the mother duck only had one left when Bella emerged holding a backpack.

"What are you bringing?" I asked out of curiosity. I hated packing with a passion. I always brought too much of one item and not enough of another. For a last-minute trip like the one we were about to take, I figured there was no way to plan it correctly.

"Our Grimoire, some candles, and a few protection charms as well as a translator amulet. I don't know about you, but I don't trust that our guide will tell us everything we need to know. He has a habit of hiding things."

I frowned. "But you trust that what he's saying about this rift is true?"

"Why would he lie?" She shrugged. "As long as the town is infected, he can't run his business. And business is the only thing he cares about."

"Not the only thing," I said with a meaningful look.

She shook her head. "He had his shot with me last night. And while I'm not proud of myself, I must admit I would have slept with him if he'd pushed for it. But he sent me home instead. He doesn't want me."

I blinked. Now wasn't the time or the place to discuss their evolving relationship, but when would we get another chance? "Hey Bells? Did you ever think that maybe the reason he didn't push was because he didn't want to pressure you before you were ready for that step? Declan cares about you. You're the only one who can't see it."

CHAPTER 9
BELLA

There was a ringing sound in my ears. That must be why I'd heard Donna wrong. My brain was trying to process her words.

Declan cares about you. You're the only one who can't see it. She didn't know what she was talking about.

You weren't there. I wanted to shout at her. There was so much I hadn't told her. Would Donna still think the demon had feelings for me if she knew about the bargain he made, how I'd cheapened myself by giving in to his mommy fetish and had been too humiliated by my reaction to meet my gaze after?

Like I was a sex-starved succubus. Or a cat in heat.

And then there was the looming accusation the demon had made. That I had somehow caused the rift. If he was right that meant I was responsible for the hallucinations. No way. Not possible. I couldn't believe it. Because I couldn't handle it.

Our conversation replayed over and over in my mind, and I still couldn't make heads or tails out of it. Only one thing kept popping up. The demon. That damn demon wanted to break me. When I'd asked how it was possible that I'd caused the rift, his explanation had been too convenient.

His words echoed in my head. "You opened that portal where no portal existed to get rid of the Servitor. But when you use demonic magic, you must pay a price of self or there will be dire consequences."

I created that portal six months ago. So why had the hallucinations just started?

He'd had an answer for that too. "I thought you understood. Until I saw how the mortals at the hotel were behaving this morning, it never occurred to me to ask. The fact that a blood relative, your sister's son, was afflicted first means your line is being punished for taking without giving."

No one had said anything about a blood sacrifice. Still reeling, I whispered, "So how do we make it right? What do I need to do to seal the rift?"

His answer chilled me to the bone. "Have your sister help you. Use her comeuppance and offer twice the sacrifice to make amends."

Twice the price. Not to mention the added cost of telling Donna that I'd fucked around with demon magic. Declan had me over a barrel and he knew it. Blame me and get me back under his demonic thumb. That was the problem with the demon. Not just the intense magic but the way he manipulated me into doing everything I promised myself that I wouldn't do. I'd sworn that I would distance myself and my children from him. I'd sworn up and down that I wouldn't let him regain the upper hand.

Yet here we sat, with him acting as puppet master and me dancing to his tune.

For all I knew, Declan had created the rift himself to get me to do whatever he wanted me to do.

And now the demon had something to hold over my head. I'd begged him not to tell Donna that the rift was my fault. Even bartered away the open-ended favor for it. *Rash, foolish Bella*. I had a spell that would have done the same job, a secret keeper spell. I could have locked the demon's lips and still have gotten the manor back.

But I'd been too panicked over the rift, the hallucinations, and the thought that I was responsible. I'd been too overwhelmed to think clearly. And Declan had once again taken shameless advantage of my innate weakness.

Evil demonic bastard.

"Bells?" Donna tipped her head to the side. "You're spacing out."

"Just thinking." Not a lie, for a change. I didn't know how the fae got by without lying. I seemed to tell a whopper twice a day.

Donna rose and handed Astrid to me. "Someone needs to be changed. And I want to go check in on Devon before we go."

As my sister's footsteps receded, I cuddled my daughter close, breathing in her sweet baby smell before heading toward the changing table. A lump formed in my throat as my hands fell into the hard-won rhythm of removing the soiled diaper, cleaning her up, and then applying the fresh one. I was by no means a natural mother. Hell, most days I doubted I was even a good mother. But I was learning. Was Donna's Comeuppance working on me already? Leaving the twins felt like a punishment for my indiscretion with the demon.

He likes you, Donna had whispered.

Liked fucking with my head.

I wouldn't go down without a fight.

With that thought in mind, I loaded the twins into their stroller and set about packing them for a week. Diapers, wipes, and rash cream. I loaded frozen milk into a cooler along with ice. Jarred pears and rice cereal went in cloth grocery bags. Teething biscuits, and toiletries, too. The list went on and on.

I changed into cargo pants, a tank top, and a zip-up sweatshirt. I packed my rucksack with a change of socks, protein bars, bottled water, a compass, and a flashlight. I added the backpack to the growing pile by the front door. One thing was for sure, my days of traveling light were over.

I spied Axel's wingspan just as I zipped the duffel bag that held onesies, socks, pants, sweaters, and hats. I didn't bother with shoes. Neither of them ever kept shoes on their feet. Just like their mother, they preferred to be barefoot. An easy way to connect with the natural world. Instead, I covered their feet with two layers of socks and blankets whenever I took them out in the cold.

My former PA didn't bother with the front door but headed for the window I'd left open. I sat on the bed, lacing up a pair of hiking boots that I'd only worn once.

"Did you find it?" I rubbed my hands on my thighs anxiously.

Axel landed and shifted into his human aspect. A distant part of me noted that I didn't recoil or even blink at the sight of his lightning wings or the monstrous cast to his skin. Was I getting used to seeing him in his fury form?

Axel pushed blond hair back from his face that glistened with sweat then turned to shut the window. "I think so. There's a weird energy surge on the far side of town from Storm Grove. I think it's coming from the old wishing well."

I knew the place he meant. The well stood on an abandoned and overgrown piece of property. Every year on our birthdays, Grand took us there to make wishes by tossing a coin down the well. None of my wishes had ever come true so I'd always assumed the well had run dry. Or just didn't work.

"We'll investigate it." I handed him the bag as well as the keys to my DeVille.

An awkward moment passed between us. Should I apologize for firing him? Or because I'd tried to separate him from Donna? My fear didn't run as strongly as it had when I'd first discovered what Axel was, but it still existed alongside the maternal instinct that demanded I keep my children safe.

Instead of making an apology I didn't feel, I decided to keep it simple. "Thank you for looking. And thank you for doing this, for taking care of my babies."

His gray gaze met mine and I was reminded of that bartender who'd looked after me after the worst night of my life. "You may not be my boss anymore, Bella, but you're still my friend."

A lump formed in my throat. I nodded.

After pocketing the keys, Axel carried the bags to the car. One trip, that's all it took the fury. I pushed the stroller. Astrid stared up at the naked tree branches that swayed in the breeze. Ember had conked out. Though I wanted to wake my son, to see his bright green eyes fixed on my face, I let him sleep. If he woke up, he'd want to eat, and it would delay their departure.

The mother's war cry—I needed my children safe more than I needed to say goodbye.

The car seats were already in place. We managed to buckle the two of them in without a fuss. I'd just snapped the last buckle on Astrid's harness when Donna rushed from the house, dropping her bag on the porch. She flung herself against Axel. When I spied the pained expression on his face, I turned away, giving them their privacy.

Finally, I understood what Donna had been saying for many months. It didn't matter what Axel could do. He was still the big-hearted guy that had driven me home after I'd been attacked. He was the PA who'd looked out for me, and the inventor of the pesto grilled cheese. He'd saved our asses more times than I could count, with the very gifts I'd condemned him for possessing.

And he made my sister happy.

A lump formed in my throat as I focused on my babies. "I love you two. And I'll get back to you as soon as I'm able."

An arm wrapped around my waist. Donna pulled me

back so Axel could shut the car door. My shoulders shook with silent sobs as he climbed behind the wheel of my Deville, reversed, and with one final wave, took my children away.

Tears tracked down my face. I'd made the right choice. The best way to keep them safe was to get them away from Storm Grove, out of Shadow Cove altogether. So why did it feel as though my heart was being put through a meat grinder? I doubled over from the pain, the crippling loss. "I can't do this."

Donna crouched beside me. "Bella, listen to me. We'll get them back. No matter what it takes, we'll get them all back."

"Are you ready?" The demon asked from behind us. I turned to face him. He was dressed head to toe in black leather. Long leather duster covered a leather vest and even leather pants and boots.

I sniffled and wiped my face, then lifted my chin before meeting those midnight eyes. "Let's do this."

Donna

I DIDN'T KNOW if it was the demon's presence or if Bella was simply determined to get this task over with so she could get her children back. I watched as she stood and then faced Declan, her jaw set. "You said there would need to be a sacrifice to close the rift. What sort of sacrifice?"

He stared at her for a long moment. "A sacrifice of self."

"Whatever it is," I stepped forward, right into the middle of the weird energy that was surging between the two of them. Their gazes shifted to fix on me. "I'll do it."

Bella shook her head. "You can't?"

"Why not?" I challenged.

The demon merely said, "We'll have to see what's necessary. Are the two of you ready?"

I held up my backpack full of first aid supplies, protein bars, and bottled water. "Good to go."

Bella gripped the straps of her backpack hard enough that her knuckles turned white and nodded.

The demon reached for her bag, but she snatched it away and then turned to face me. "Let's take your car."

I blinked at Declan's oversized SUV that would easily fit all of us offroad but recovered quickly. My sister was probably feeling the need to exert control. I couldn't blame her. More impressive was that Declan didn't argue about the choice. He just watched Bella closely, almost as if he understood the strain the past few minutes had put on her.

Did he? I knew the demon was learning. He asked bizarre questions while we'd gone over plans for redesigning the manor. Things like what games Bella and I had played as a child and what the point of Taco Tuesday was. "To eat tacos on Tuesdays," seemed like a straightforward answer. But he'd probed until I finally said, "I think the idea is to give you something to look forward to."

That had made those dark brows draw together.

We headed toward my Impala. Bella slid into the back, leaving shotgun to Declan. It was bizarre having the large male form in my commuter mobile. I'd driven the sedan with everything from rugs to rocking chairs to rolls of wallpaper and bins of rubbish, but none of them took up as much room as the demon.

"Head out to the main road that circles the lake," Declan instructed.

From time to time, I glanced in the rearview mirror to check on Bella. She stared out the window, saying nothing. Her green eyes were red-rimmed If it had been anything but my son's life on the line I would have told the demon that Bella wasn't up to this. She'd been dealing with too much, including her feelings for him.

I studied the demon, too. He sat beside me, tense as anything. There was something about the way his gaze shifted, and his hands pressed into his thighs. Every muscle was strung tight, almost as though he was bracing for a hit. Odd, I was a solid driver, much better than Bella. Was it just being chauffeured around that unnerved him or was there something more at work?

"Turn here," Declan pointed to a rutted dirt road. I took the sharp left, and we bumped along the road that wound through the pines and budding maples. It would be weeks yet before the mighty oaks leafed out and shaded this space. The recent rain had mud spattering the Impala. I skidded twice but managed to catch it before losing control entirely.

We bounced along for almost two miles before coming to a fork in the road. I slowed to a stop and then muttered, "Which way?"

The demon picked something out of his shirt and held it aloft. A pendulum, I realized, though it was unlike any of the ones Bella and I had used as children. It pulsed with an eerie green light almost as though a lightning bug had been trapped within the stone but still sent its bioluminescent signals.

"What is that?" It was the first time Bella had spoken since leaving the manor.

"A shadow stone," The demon studied it as it twisted on the leather cord. He moved it from the left path then over to the right.

"Right," Declan said as the stone glowed brighter toward the right-hand fork.

I tugged on the wheel, and we went right.

"Where did you get it?" Bella asked from the back seat.

"The demonic realm," Declan tucked the shadow stone back under his long-sleeved black

button down and then turned in the seat, wedging his wide shoulders so he could face both of us. "It's a rite of passage for any who can be summoned to chip a section off the stone. It allows us to sense portals to the underworld."

"How many portals are there?" I asked.

"Hundreds sprinkled across the globe. Most of them sealed, like the one at Storm Grove." He cast Bella a glance. "Portals are created with a very specific spell, almost like a rubber stopper that allows things to be added into the demon plane but never removed from it. A rift is different. It's a two-way street. Worse things than wraiths can escape through a rift."

"Like whatever's causing the hallucinations?" I asked.

He nodded just as the trees parted into a flat expanse. I spied the remains of a stone wall.

My foot tapped the brake and I slowed to examine it. "It looks like the foundation for an old house."

Bella leaned forward to study it. "It must have belonged to whoever used this well, originally."

"The well should be just up ahead." Declan pointed. "We can walk from here."

We exited the car and strode through the overgrown field. I could make out the outline of the well. It stood by itself on the top of the hill. It was one of the covered ones with an oversized roof that protected the pully system and bucket from eroding. The little thatched roof was littered with vines and moss grew between the stones The wooden well cover had rotted away. A snarl of weeds spilled out of the opening, giving the place a whimsical look, like a window into a simpler time.

The oddness though came from the eerie green light that spilled out from the mouth of the well.

"What was it Grand always said about this place?" I asked Bella as we climbed the hill.

"If you tossed in a coin and heard the sound of it hitting bottom, the wish of your heart would come true." She smiled a little and then began fiddling with her cross-body bag.

"What are you doing?" Declan asked as he watched her stride up to the very lip of the well.

Bella didn't answer. Instead, I saw her shoulders rise and fall. Her hand extended out from her body. There was a flash of light as something reflected the sun. A coin. She dropped it and then leaned forward, bracing her hands on the lip of the well. I held my breath, listening, willing the simple solution to be the one that worked.

"It was worth a try," I said to her when it became clear that her wish hadn't affected the green light. Wouldn't it have been great if all our troubles vanished because Bella wished them away? Sadly, even magic didn't tie everything up with a nice little bow.

Bella shrugged and then turned her attention to Declan. "What do we do now?"

A shot of cold zipped along my spine as his irises flamed with the red and orange fire. He bent down and shrugged his pack off, then pulled out the rope. "Now we climb down until we locate the rift."

CHAPTER 10
BELLA

"That's really not safe," Donna took a step forward, as though to stop the demon. "Old hand-dug wells can be a hundred feet deep and can collapse in on themselves. What if it collapses on top of us?"

"It's a risk," the demon didn't pause in his work. "But there's no other way to get to where we need to go."

"Can't you just magic us down there?" I asked. My palms were coated with sweat, and I couldn't seem to take a full breath.

"There's no telling how my magic will respond so close to a rift. We could end up buried alive." Declan was busy driving stakes into the ground around the well.

I exchanged a look with Donna. She did a palms-up gesture. "When he puts it that way, climbing might be our best option."

The sunlight was fading. I tried to imagine climbing down as the circle of sky over the top of the well grew smaller and smaller. Like being swallowed by some huge hungry beast. My stomach heaved. If what the demon said about magic backfiring so near an open rift was true, I'd have no defense down there. And that was before I made whatever sacrifice I needed to close the rift.

"I have to pee," I announced and marched off toward the tree line.

Unfortunately, Donna was hot on my heels. "You okay?"

"Not even a little," I bent at the waist and braced my hands on my knees.

"It's just like climbing the rope in gym class." My sister said.

My gaze met hers. "Yeah, I never managed more than three knots."

"Me neither." She grimaced. "Okay, so maybe that isn't the best solution. But it looks like Declan brought some gear so maybe we'll manage okay?"

I didn't answer, my thoughts whirled around and around as I imagined the maw of the earth swallowing me whole.

"I can do it," Donna put her hand on the back of my neck and squeezed. "Bella, it's okay. I can make the sacrifice."

It's not yours to make! I didn't say it out loud though my brain shrieked the words. This was my fault, my mistake. I hadn't known what I was doing and now we were going to climb down the freaking wishing well to make a sacrifice. And we both had to go. Donna needed to use her comeuppance on me.

Somehow, I found the strength to stand upright. "We need to stick together. We're stronger together, right?"

Her emerald green gaze roved over my face. Then she nodded. "Right. Well, I really do have to pee."

"Me too." The joys of middle age, especially after carrying twins.

We parted to deal with our bodily functions. I made it back to the well first in time to see the demon tinkering with what looked like a harness.

"Come here, witchling. Try this on for size." The tone was far from his usual smooth banter.

I stepped forward, glad I'd taken the time to change into pants as I stepped through the leg holes of the harness. Declan pulled the bits up and then circled around behind me.

"Are you all right?" I asked him as he tightened a strap behind me.

His fingers hesitated. "I don't like being so near to the rift."

That explained why his gaze darted as though he was hunting for an escape.

"Tell me more about the sacrifice," I put my hand over his as he reached around me to fiddle with the harness. "That way you don't need to go down there."

He held still a moment then moved around to look into my eyes. "Demon magic takes from the wielder. It especially likes unique things. Anything from a natural talent to your most cherished memories, to years taken off mortal life."

"Years?" I swallowed.

"One or two perhaps. I've never seen a spell that costs more than five."

"And you've been doing this for centuries?" I stared at him, trying to wrap my brain around it.

"Some believe the reason we have no identity is that magic has consumed us all. Trying to bleed away all the things that make us unique, one spell at a time."

"I'm sorry." The words popped out before I could think them through.

"So am I, witchling. It would have gone easier on you if you'd paid in advance. Now we don't know the cost."

Declan turned away just as Donna reemerged from the woods. She'd tucked her flannel shirt into her waistband and was studying the harness I wore dubiously.

"You're sure we'll be able to get back up?" She asked.

The demon held the loops of the leg holes for her the same way he'd done for me. "That remains to be seen."

"Fantastic," my sister muttered.

I stared at the well while Donna got situated. No one said a word, each of us lost in our own thoughts. I felt as though we ought to be hatching some sort of plan. Declan had the knowledge, I had the magic and Donna had the power to make me pay for my mistake.

She just didn't know it yet.

"Want me to go first?" My sister asked.

I tugged on the gloves Declan had provided me with and shook my head. "No. I will."

Declan handed me a helmet with a lantern on top, the kind miners wore when going into the mouth of the cave.

I cleared a section of brambles and decaying vines off

the edge of the well, then shook the side. The stone held tight, so I sat on it and then donned my helmet before swinging my legs over. The light got lost in the green glow that seemed to reach on and on and on.

"Okay," I breathed and then braced my feet on the side of the well. Nothing crumbled and the intricate line system the demon had rigged held my full weight. "So far so good."

Declan's irises danced with fire. "Be careful, witchling. The contamination causing the hallucinations might not be the only thing that has crossed over."

I met his gaze nodded and then took a step down. Then another. I didn't look up at either of them, instead focusing my attention on the section below me. More vines and moss grew on the inside part of the well. They glowed in the eerie green light. My boots slipped a few times as I did my horizontal walk down into the well, skidding on wet slime and stone.

Hand-dug wells in our area usually didn't go much beyond twenty feet. We had plenty of rain so oftentimes the water table was easier to reach. Add to that the rocky terrain that had been tough to dig through. I kept expecting to see the bottom. When I didn't, I glanced back up to see how far I'd come.

The fading daylight spilled in through the mouth of the well that looked about the size of a quarter. I could barely make out the two faces that peered down at me.

"I'm okay," I called up to Declan and Donna. My voice bounced off the sides of the well.

"Do you see anything yet?" my twin asked. "Anything out of the ordinary?"

"Other than the toxic green light?" I tried my best not to think about radon and other forms of radiation that could leech out from these rocks. Tried to focus on the end goal. Healing the rift, making the sacrifice. Getting Devon well and getting my babies back.

The light on my head flickered and went out.

"Damn it, demon," I muttered. "What sort of cheap-ass helmet did you...?"

My words trailed off as I smelled it.

Sulfur.

I'd found the rift.

~

Donna

"I'm at the bottom!" Bella shouted. Her voice sounded very far away.

Which meant it was my turn. As she always did, my twin made climbing down into the well look like it was no big deal. Only someone who knew her as well as I did could have read the terror she'd kept locked down tight.

"What do you see?" Declan leaned over the edge to call out to her.

"A green sludge. And a shitload of coins," Bella called back.

I snorted. "Guess we weren't the only ones making wishes in a dried-up well."

The demon didn't even glance my way. His entire body was tense, his eyes burning.

"I'm surprised you didn't get a helmet cam," I said as I positioned myself to start walking down the well.

"Magic and technology don't always play well together. Especially rogue demon magic. You should know that, Donna Sanders-Allen."

"Just Donna," I corrected and then took my first step.

There was a ping as though something had snapped off and then I felt the tension on the rope attached to my harness give way. The demon lunged for the pully that had snapped. I watched in horror as it slid through his grip.

The rope unspooled. I fell.

I was too stunned to scream as I descended into the earth. My heart was lodged in my throat, cutting off my air. Bella. I was going to land on top of Bella and we'd both be killed.

Would two unintended deaths be enough of a sacrifice to close the rift?

The rope snagged, jolting me to a sudden stop. I gasped and my shoulder collided with the side of the well. I hung suspended like a teabag on the verge of being dunked.

"Donna!" Two voices shouted, one from above and the other from several yards below.

"What. The. Shit. Demon?" I shouted when I had air.

"Sorry!" he called back, sounding as if he was apologizing for backing into my car, not nearly dropping me to my death.

"Are you okay?" Bella hollered.

"Been better." Of course, it could have been much worse too. "Am I okay to keep going?"

"Probably," Declan said.

"Not exactly reassuring." I wondered if Axel had felt my terror. I hoped he wouldn't come here. He had to protect the twins.

I took a tentative step. Then another. My headlamp flickered and then went out.

"More magic and technology issues," I grumbled. "Bella?"

"Here." She sounded much closer than she had before. "I'm pretty sure the demon is just a cheapskate."

I was glad she was able to make light—so to speak— of the two of us being trapped down a well. "Is there enough room for me down there with you?"

The hole itself was narrow. When my boots pressed against the north side I could have reached out with my fingertips and brushed the south side of the well.

"More than," Bella replied. "It gets wider the deeper you go."

"Any water?" I asked as I trekked down a few more feet."

"Not unless you count the ooze."

"The ooze?" I dared to peak over one shoulder toward the sound of her voice and that's when I spotted it.

The yellow-green glow just like the light trapped in Declan's pendulum, spilled through a crevice in the dirt wall. Bella stood directly before it, up to her ankles in the gunk. The light from the ooze made her pale skin look sickly. She'd removed her gloves and her hands hovered over the light.

"Bella! Don't touch it!" I warned.

She glanced up and then stepped back. Still horizontal, I goose-stepped around the green gunk until my feet touched the bottom.

"So now what?" Dizziness crested over me at the feeling of standing vertically once more. Or maybe it was the ooze. "If we can't use magic, then how do we make a sacrifice?"

"We need to connect with it," my sister murmured. Bella bent down and pulled something out of her boot. It was a small knife with a black handle.

I didn't like the way the green glow seemed to highlight the blade. "What do you mean, connect?"

"Tap your comeuppance," Bella said.

I glared at her. "Declan said we shouldn't use magic down here."

"Just trust me, Donna." She winced as the knife cut into her skin. In the green light, the blood looked almost black.

I was getting a sick feeling in my stomach. Like when we'd been kids and I'd been left out of the magic and the decisions. But I wasn't a dud anymore. "Bella, what aren't you telling me?"

She held my gaze. "I need you to use your comeuppance on me. It's the only way to seal this rift."

My lips parted. "I can't."

Her hand was clenched in a fist, holding the blood within. "You can. You're a legacy. Reach out to the universe and let whatever happens happen."

I didn't like the sound of that. "But what if—"

"Do you want Devon back?" she snapped.

"Of course."

"Then do it." Her green eyes appeared to glow in the eerie light.

I reached down into the ground. Magic thrummed through me like a bass drum. Buried in the Earth this way, grounding was almost effortless. The phantom wind from the astral plane began to swirl around us and I reached for the brilliant thread deep inside myself, that was part of my fabric, my make-up. My innate power, comeuppance.

I never knew what it would do when I grasped that thread. Who it would affect. Down here, there were just the two of us.

Bella's fingers uncurled and she reached for the rift, determined to pay the price. For me and for Devon and all of Shadow Cove.

I plucked the string. It reverberated through me.

Bella collapsed to the ground, screaming.

CHAPTER 11
DONNA

The sounds of Bella's shrieks ripped at my heart. Her hand still bled. She crumpled like a wet paper bag, falling onto her side into the green ooze. Heedless of my aching body after the jarring fall, I fell to my knees beside her. "Bella?"

A hand gripped my wrist before I could roll her onto her back. "Don't touch her."

I stared up and up into Declan's burning eyes. "What's happening to her?"

He didn't answer, though he did let go of my wrist. I didn't reach for Bella again although her screams would haunt me forever.

"We can't just leave her like this. How do we help her?"

"You can't," Declan said. If I had just met him, I would have thought he was indifferent to the sobbing woman on the ground at his feet. But the tightness of his jaw gave him away. "All you can do is tend to her when she comes out of it."

"When—?" The ground lurched beneath our feet. I careened and would have collapsed on top of Bella, but the demon caught me.

"What's happening?"

He was muttering something indistinct and between the trembling world around us and Bella's continued shrieks, I couldn't hear. The demon crouched beside my sister and then held out a hand to me. I took it.

The ooze along the floor seemed to expand and pulse with more intensity. Stones fell from above. I flinched as they bounced off an invisible shield above our heads. I shouted at Declan. "Are you crazy? Get us out of here!"

"I can't not until it's done."

"This place is a death trap," I hollered.

He glared up at me. "If we leave now her sacrifice will be in vain. Do you want that?"

No, I didn't. Neither did I want to be squished if his demonic shielding gave out. Then I remembered what he'd said. "Wait, you said we shouldn't use magic down here!"

Declan didn't respond but the well did. A jagged green line carved itself along the well's Eastern wall, glowing far brighter than the ooze. It seemed to thrum with life. I stared at it, transfixed. Everything else faded to background noise. Bella's cries, the rumbling of the ground, even my worry for Devon. The ooze reached for us, tendrils snaking up from the pit as though the stuff was sentient. I wanted to move but the light transfixed me to the spot.

A sudden flash made me throw up an arm to shield my eyes. I was tossed into Declan, who caught me before

my head could strike the ground. Bella had quit screaming, at least. Somehow I didn't think our situation had
improved.

"What happened?" I rasped.

His dark eyes were full of panic. He reached out and
black smoke emanated from his hands. The second it hit
the ooze, the stuff crumbled to ash. He brushed it off of
Bella who still lay on her side, trembling. "We need to get
out of here. Now."

Sounded like a plan to me. Declan reached for Bella's
ankle and flinched at the contact. He shut his eyes.

Nothing happened.

"No," the demon growled. His face scrunched with
concentration. "No!"

"What?" My vision was blurred after the flash of
light. The demon set me aside and withdrew from Bella,
who mercifully had quieted down. "What's the matter?"

Setting me aside, Declan rose and went to the wall
with the carved line. It appeared inverted, as though it
was a reflection in a mirror. He touched it. Then slapped
it. His hands curled up into fists and he battered it with
all his strength.

"Hey!" Though I was shaky on my feet, I moved to
intercept him. Bodily blocking the wall that had been
winning the boxing match I caught his arms, before he
could beat himself bloody. "Declan, stop. What's
wrong?"

"You don't understand," the demon ripped free of my
grasp and ran a hand through his hair.

"You're right, I don't. Tell me what the hell
happened?"

"What happened is we've been sucked through the rift." Declan held my gaze and I swear I've never felt so cold in my life as when I his burning irises as he spoke the words, "We're trapped in the demonic underworld."

Bella

It's not real.

My entire body ached, from the beating they'd given me. I'd never felt so helpless, so powerless. I was a witch, a legacy from a proud family line. I should have been safe, should have been able to protect myself from them.

He's dead. The thought came and was ushered out by the sound of mocking male laughter. The burning humiliation. The fear....

I crawled on my hands and knees. My clothes were gone. Left behind in my hurry to leave a terrible place. I didn't know where I was, or how far from town. From help.

Hands gripped me by the ankles and dragged me backward. I shrieked as I lost the ground I'd made, was hauled up over a shoulder, and carried up the stairs into that place. The farmhouse.

That's not how it happened.

The stray thoughts of logic drifted outside my mind. They broke like cobwebs under the chainsaw of terror that carved through me as I clawed and kicked and cried. No more. I couldn't take any more.

"Bella!"

A woman's voice. Familiar. Safe. I looked around but could only see them...

Zeke. He shook me hard, so hard my skull bounced off the ground. White hot pain exploded behind my eyes. He backhanded me across the jaw. I could taste blood but didn't dare spit it out. He liked the sight of my blood, it excited him. Like a shark smelling it in the water.

He shoved his pants down, his hand moving between my legs.

"Not again," I moaned. I couldn't take it. Knew I would break if he did it again. He'd already seen me cry, beg, bleed. My magic failed me. I had no defenses as he...

"Witchling!"

The image of Zeke Bradburry faded at the sound of that voice. Like the woman's but much stronger. Safer. I drifted in darkness, hunting for that voice, the one that had pulled me from that horrible dream.

No, not a dream. It had been like that the night the Bradburys had lured me onto their territory. They'd bound my powers. Made me cry and beg and bleed.

Gradually I could feel something. The warmth of another's flesh pressed against mine. It dissipated the cold that ran through my body from head to foot. I groaned and reached toward it. I needed more. Anything to displace the bone-shattering cold.

"I think she's coming around." The woman's voice. Donna.

"Bella," the man muttered. "Can you hear me?"

I wanted to see his face. To see those eyes and know he was real. That it wasn't some sort of trick the Bradbury's were playing. Throwing out a life preserver just to watch me flail.

Though my eyelids felt as though they weighed ten thousand pounds, I forced them up. Just to slits. Just so I could see.

The green glow surrounded him, but brighter than that were the flames in his dark irises. "Declan?" I whispered.

He traced my cheek with a gentle caress. "There you are, witchling. Are you all right?"

"No." I croaked. "What are you doing down here?"

He didn't answer. Instead, he looked over at Donna. "I think she'll be all right."

I scowled as I looked up past him. There was no rope, no opening to the well. Just what looked like icicles. I could see my breath with every exhale.

Where were we? It was colder than it had been at the bottom of the well. Much colder. Instead of the ooze coming from just one spot, it seemed to drip from the icicles and slither down a shield that curved above our heads.

"Our brilliant friend here did exactly what he told us not to do," Donna murmured from behind me. "He poofed himself down to the bottom of the well. And the next thing you know we were being sucked into the fissure. Do you think you can drink?"

My lips were cracked and dry and my tongue had swollen up to three times its normal size. I thought I could still taste the metallic tang of blood but that might be the lingering effects from the nightmare. Plus, my teeth were chattering.

Declan held me tighter. "It will warm in a few moments. I cast a body heat containment spell around this niche to keep us from freezing." He vowed and shifted me up against his chest until I was in an upright position with little of my body in contact with the frigid stone.

My limbs felt limp and weak, as though I were awakening from a long illness. "How long was I out?"

"We're not sure," Donna said as she crouched beside me. "At least two days."

I'd just taken a sip of water and choked as it slid down the wrong pipe. "Two days?"

"Drink," Declan murmured and held the water bottle to my lips.

I took a small sip. It was the single best thing I'd ever tasted. I drank more until the demon pulled it away and screwed the cap back on.

"We're running low," he cautioned. "We're going need to find another source of potable water soon."

The heat that radiated off him kept the cold at bay. I leaned against him as though he were the best body pillow in the world. Of their own volition, my eyelids drifted shut.

"Is she all right?" Donna's voice drifted like pollen through the spring air.

"She will be." I could feel Declan's long fingers running through my hair. "Let her rest awhile longer and then we'll start looking for a portal."

"I thought you said the portals are one way?" Donna murmured.

"They are unless one is summoned. And if the rift is

sealed, then your fury will return to Shadow Cove and be hunting for a way to get you back. The closest portal to Storm Grove is our best bet for escape."

They were quiet then. Weariness overcame me. We were in the damned demonic underworld. The place that I'd summoned the demon from all those months ago. The demon who made me feel safe.

He'd come for me. He hadn't wanted to. Declan hated the demon plane. Had bartered with us so he'd never have to return to this place. And yet, he'd entered the well to help me. To protect me.

My feelings defied logic. It had been this way with him since the beginning. Something about him beckoned me. Even when he hadn't been fully formed. Even when I thought he'd been after my children for some horrible demonic rite, I'd been drawn to him. Was it just the allure of the bad boy? Somehow, I didn't think so.

I'd experienced evil. The recollection made me curve tighter to the demon. I floated once more, too exhausted to hold a thought.

"What did you see, witchling?" I felt his fingers in my hair.

"Huh?"

"When you touched the rift. What was it you saw?"

I shook my head, not willing to talk about it.

"It might help us find a way out," those fingers continued to stroke, to lull me into a languid stupor.

"Donna?" I slit one eye to see if she was watching.

"She's gone to look for water," Declan murmured. "Tell me what you saw."

"Zeke," I whispered and heard the demon swear. "He came after me and dragged me back into the farmhouse."

"The farmhouse you sent here," Declan breathed. "That was your price. You dropped something that didn't belong in this place. And the memory of what happened there will gnaw at you."

My nails dug into his forearm. "You say that like it isn't over."

"It's not. At least not as long as we're here. If you use large magic, like reflection, that memory will come for you. It's taking your inner strength. That's the price you must pay."

A soft whimper escaped. "How do I fight it?"

"You can't," Declan stroked my cheek. "Not here. This entire plane is designed to strip us down for parts."

I couldn't help it then. Couldn't stop the tears from spilling over, or my body from shaking. I couldn't live through that again. I wouldn't survive it.

He petted my hair again. "Be at ease, witchling. Your sister is looking for a way out of here. And seeing what Donna-Sanders Allen is capable of is a wonderous thing to behold."

CHAPTER 12
DONNA

As hell planes went, the demonic underworld was first-rate. The sulfur stank was fading, or more likely, after two days, I was just getting used to it. The green light and the endless cold made every muscle in my body ache. The gut-clenching need to get out, to return to Devon and contact Axel drove me forward and kept me thinking about the one thing I really couldn't afford to dwell on.

That my mother had died here.

A memory rose. The feeling of falling through the portal at Storm Grove. Of sensing an echo of her presence. Mom. She'd sacrificed herself to keep the portal closed. She hadn't had Axel to catch her or Declan to show her the way out. I felt her in that endless drop.

And some part of me could feel her still.

It was nuts, I was a grown-ass woman with a child of my own. Yet not a day went by that I didn't think of her. And I could admit to myself at least that I'd been so caught up in Axel and Bella and the twins, that I hadn't properly dealt with the feelings knowing my mother hadn't abandoned us had stirred.

"Look at me being all self-actualized and shit," I muttered as I turned yet another corner in the glowing green labyrinth. Shadow stone, Declan had called it. The same thing was in his pendulum. The piece of the underworld that had been given to him when he'd fought his way to the top, proved himself to be a demon who could ensnare magical practitioners who didn't know what they were doing in bargains designed to get them killed.

I paused with one hand, covered in spare socks, and leaned against the icy wall. Grand had taught us the history of demons and witches. That history didn't match up with the version Declan had laid out while Bella had been unconscious.

Witches believed in maintaining balance. They gave to their community as they took and never interfered with free will. But some had skirted that line too closely. Had done harm for their own self-interest. After the witch trials had ravaged Europe, those who had pushed one too many boundaries were banished to a hell plane. There they would remain.

The banished, who'd called themselves demons, hadn't been content with their world. They'd created the wraiths, the spirits who could cross through and take over unwary mortals. Forever seeking a way to open the portals so they could retaliate against the ones who'd tossed them aside.

Back when I'd first heard the story my response had been the same as any witch-child's. I'd feared the demons and the idea they would ever return. Mom had too. Why else would she have given her life to trap them in this horrible place?

Had the demons done horrific things? Of course. But after speaking with Declan, I saw the situation in a new light.

"This plane doesn't rehabilitate demons. It feeds on us a little bit at a time. It steals everything from us. Taste. Smell. Physical characteristics. Some demons lose pigment in their eyes and hair. Only a few precious memories to help us cling to who we are."

"But if magic is what causes you to lose all of that why use it?" I'd asked.

He gestured toward the shield that was keeping out the worst of the cold. "Because we would die without magic. If the cold doesn't get us, starvation or dehydration will. It's a matter of survival."

He'd held his pendant aloft. "You see this stone? It reminds me of where I come from. The deal my mother made with a mortal. It was at his request. He begged her to help. So, she did. And that one act is what sealed our fate."

"How old were you?" I'd whispered.

"Six." He turned away, leaving me to absorb his words.

Instead of rehabilitating the demons, witches had tossed them away. Kicked the problem under the rug out of self-interest. Was that a trait of a compassionate race? And they still did it. Any witch caught using demonic magic was banished to the realm. Even children.

I'd lashed out with comeuppance and burned the flesh from the bones of the demons who'd been waiting to cross. To escape this place that stole everything they were. Was I any better than the sanctimonious witches who'd responded out of fear?

There were no answers. And there was no freaking water. All we had was my supply pack. I either needed to find a way to contact Axel so he could open a portal or find a source of drinking water.

I took yet another turn and came to a series of caves. The light from my headlamp had cracked, but it still worked. I shone it in. Glowing white stalactites dripped what looked like water. At least it wasn't the ooze that kept collecting on my climbing helmet. I studied the pools. Though the glow from the rocks made it seem as though the liquid shone, I thought that perhaps the color was reflective only. After all, demons managed to survive in the hell realm for hundreds of years. They couldn't have if there was nothing to drink.

I retrieved my canteen and held it under the dripping stone. It took several minutes to fill even halfway. I brought it to my nose and sniffed. Nothing. Setting the water bottle on an outcropping of rock, I used a lighter to heat the bottle, listening for the telltale boiling sound. If I could boil off any impurities that would leave us with drinking water.

I hoped.

"What are you doing in here?"

Startled, I whirled around at the voice. In my clumsiness, I knocked the metal bottle to the floor and all the precious liquid glugged out onto the stone. I couldn't breathe as I beheld the demon in front of me.

The being in the cave stood almost seven feet tall. It

was obvious the creature had been feeding the hell plane for a very long time. Its features were sunken, had no hair, and its eyes faded to a bland whitish color. It looked like a cavefish, down to the pasty skin that peeked out from tattered rags.

"Are you trying to poison a foe?" The demon asked me. "Or have you had enough and are foolishly trying to take your own life? There are quicker ways than dying from the toxic cave milk."

I glanced from the demon to the canteen and back. "I didn't know. I was thirsty and I thought—"

To my surprise, the demon chuckled. "New here, are you? What are you in for?"

"Stupidity," I muttered.

The demon laughed once more. "Aren't we all? Well, those of us who remain after the conflagration."

"Conflagration?" I asked.

The demon waved it away. "No matter. Do you have a name still or did those bastards on the magic council strip your memories?"

"They do that?" It was on the tip of my tongue to tell the creature before me that the magic council had been disbanded but hesitated. If the demons knew that our world had devolved into the Wild West, who knows what they would do?

"You are young. Yes, they did that to those they feared would retaliate. And with no memories to cling to this place gets to you that much sooner." The demon shook its head. "Like it doesn't already claim all we have and more. But there are worse things. Come with me, Newling, I'll show you around."

THE DEMON TOOK me to a clear spring that bubbled up from a crack in the green stone. The water reeked of sulfur but watching my host drink greedily directly from the source I decided to roll the dice. The water didn't taste any better than it smelled, but it parched my dry throat. At the demon's warning, I left the canteen that had the drippings from the toxic cave behind not wanting to experience the agonizing death that was promised. But I did have Bella's canteen still and filled it to the brim.

I had a decision to make. Bella and Declan needed water too. Should I tell my new guide about them? I feared this demon would recognize Declan. What if they were rivals? What if we couldn't protect Bella, who was still weak from whatever happened at the bottom of the well?

Not worth the risk. "Well, I appreciate your showing me this place, but I should probably get going."

"Going?" The demon crouched on a rock and tilted its head to look at me. "Going where?"

I shrugged.

"That's what I thought. You'll want to stick with me, Newling. The predators come out at night."

I glanced around. The only source of light emanated from the stone, and it appeared just as bright as when we first arrived. "How can you tell day from night?"

"Practice." The demon lept down and landed with fluid grace by my side. There wasn't a spare ounce of fat on its body. "Come on, we'll find a shelter and hunker in for the night."

Unable to think of a plausible excuse, I did as the demon suggested.

It soon became clear that I wouldn't be able to find Bella and Declan again if I tried. I got lost in the town where I had lived my whole life. My wonky brain and piss-poor sense of direction didn't stand a chance as one trail bled into another and there was nothing to distinguish one from another.

"How can you tell where you're going?" I huffed. Unlike the demon I was not all muscle and sinew and the constant trekking over rocky terrain stole my breath.

"Practice," my guide said.

That wasn't much help. Still, I followed in their wake.

Suddenly the stone parted to reveal a forest glade. But the trees looked nothing like the pines and hickory trees from back home. Instead, they appeared to be made from overcooked green noodles. The closest comparison my brain could make was a weeping willow with sturdier branches. They too reeked of sulfur and a sticky sap ran down the trunk.

"Don't touch the sap," the demon told me. "It's acidic and will burn the flesh from your bones."

I jerked my sock-covered hand away in the nick of time. Was everything in this horrible place designed to torture?

The demon wound through the trees with effortless grace and then pointed to a small rocky outcropping that jutted above the tree line. "There's a shelter. Climb the trees up but make sure not to break any of the branches."

"Because of the acid sap. Got it." I worried that my weight would prove too much for the noodle trees, but there didn't appear to be any sort of alternative. The demon went first, scrambling like a monkey up through the boughs. My guide hefted up over the outer edge of the lip and then stood atop it not even a full minute later.

I swallowed and readjusted my hand socks. Though I doubted there'd be enough protection should I inadvertently contact the sap, it was better than having my bare skin touch it. Taking a deep breath, I began to climb.

"Newling, you are a slowpoke!" the demon chortled from the rocky outcropping. "I'm beginning to think you *want* the Bane to eat you."

"What's a bane?" I didn't care, was only half listening. My focus had to be on the climb, where to grasp, and where to plant my feet.

Suddenly a piercing cry tore through the forest. Then the ground began to shake. Not like the earthquake before the rift had sucked us through. This was intermittent like a great beast the size of a T-Rex taking massive steps in succession. *Boom. Boom. Boom.*

"That is the Bane." The demon daggled sinewy legs over the edge of the outcropping. "Better hurry up before it catches your scent. The Bane always prefers fresh meat that doesn't stink of brimstone."

No time. I had no time. I was forty-five years old for fuck's sake. Even if my only athletic activity hadn't been channel surfing, there was no way I was up to outrunning a massive predator that could make the ground shake.

Frantic, I scrambled up to the next noodle branch. It

held and using my legs against the tree trunk I pushed myself up farther. The sound of sizzling met my ears. I jerked my foot out of the dribble of sap I'd stepped in. The Bane shrieked again. Closer. Even if each booming step hadn't heralded its approach, the way the blood pumped through my veins told me to hurry. To get my well-padded backside up the tree and to the outcropping.

Bella would never know what happened to me. Why hadn't gone back to them? Why hadn't I sent Declan out to search for water instead of getting myself into a predicament? Because I'd insisted that he stay to hold the shield and keep Bella from freezing to death. If he cared for her at all, he'd keep her safe until they found a way back to our world.

Ten feet to go. I scrambled and climbed. Then was sucked vertical as an enormous *thing*, drew in a massive breath, creating a hurricane-force gust as it exhaled.

Shaken, I held completely still. Through the noodle limbs, I spotted the Bane. It was lovely, in a terrifying kind of way. It had a hood like a king Cobra though its face was covered in golden fur. It walked on two beefy legs covered with scales. Its arms appeared to be bone-less. They undulated and struck out at the noodle trees like whips. It's eyes though, that were the most unnerving thing. It was like a goat with vertical pupils that flamed the same way Declan's did when he was angry.

It didn't see me, but it sniffed again, the slit-like nostrils expanding so it could suck all the air in from the surrounding forest. I hung on to the noodle branch for dear life even as my body was tossed about like a bottle in the ocean. My heart pounded in my chest. I thought I might faint. Better to fall to my death than to be dinner for that monstrous creature.

Above me, the demon who'd been guiding me made a sort of chuffing sound. My eyes went wide as the Bade swung its head in that direction. Then the demon through a rock back in the direction we'd come. A chorus of yowls erupted and what looked like a dozen orange and brown lizards skittered out of the noodle trees. The massive beast screeched once more and then stormed off after the scurrying prey.

My hands were drenched in sweat but somehow I managed to hold on to the noodle limb. The demon crouched over me, extending a long, thin arm, and helped haul my weary carcass up onto the outcropping.

"Thank you." The words popped out before I could think better of them. Thanking a fae was like admitting you owed it a favor. Was the same true for demons?

My guide merely shrugged. "It's been a long time since I had anyone to talk to."

"What were those things you disturbed?"

"Grugs," The demon shrugged. "They're one of the few things we can eat around here. I spotted the nest on my ascent, but figured you'd rather go hungry and let them be dinner for the Bane instead."

"You figured right," I shut my eyes and then shivered against the stone floor.

"Come on, Newling. I'll teach you how to build a fire." My guide offered me a hand up and I took it.

CHAPTER 13
BELLA

"Witchling, we need to tell your sister what's going on," Declan murmured in my ear. "I believe she'll understand why you felt the need to keep her in the dark. But she might come up with a solution we've missed."

My whole body shuddered. The cold, exhaustion, emotional and magical overwhelm. All of it was taking its toll. Arguing with the demon was pointless so I just nestled closer to him, trying to let his warmth seep through the layers of clothes that separated us.

He was being so gentle. The way he held me and stroked my hair almost as if he...cared. I knew it wasn't real. Declan didn't care. He'd made that clear enough the night he'd touched me, then sent me out of his sight, like a sex worker in an Uber.

The demon picked up my hands and studied my fingertips. His perfectly sculpted dark brows drew together. The flames in his irises blazed hotter as he met my gaze. "This isn't working. You're suffering hypothermia. I need to strip you."

"A.... likely...story." I chattered.

He set me down and moved back enough to remove his leather duster. The corner of his aristocratic mouth kicked up as he reached for my jacket. "Don't you trust me?"

Not as far as I could throw you. I couldn't speak through and curled tighter into myself. He laid out his clothes on the ground before reaching for me. "Skin-to-skin contact is the

best way to stay warm. Didn't you ever go camping?"

I shook my head. he plucked me up like a daisy, stood me on his discarded clothes, and began unbuttoning my flannel overshirt. He left it on but open as he reached for the jeans I was fumbling with. "Stop. Bella. Let me."

I shook harder as he did, my hands balling into fists. I had never been so cold in my life. Or felt so helpless.

Declan left my socks and underwear on as he laid me down and spooned up against my back. He moved and shifted around reaching for other clothing items to concoct a makeshift blanket.

At first, I didn't feel a difference. Then the warmth of the arm draped over me, and the muscled torso that pressed into my back began to seep through. My thoughts grew foggy as he squeezed me even tighter into him.

"Better?" Declan murmured.

"Yes." The heat that radiated from him and through me was incredible. Unlike sitting before a fire, where one side was too hot, the other always cold, his internal flame licked through me, heating my blood so it pumped faster, warming my extremities.

He nuzzled my hair. "You smell *wonderful*."

That one word made me melt deeper into him. I arched against him, wanting to sink farther into his caress.

That warm comforting hand that I was relying on for survival suggestively slid across my belly. "There's an even better way to keep you warm."

I could feel him hard and hot against my backside. And judging from the imprint he had zero problem with shrinkage.

Not happening. That's what I should have said. *Go fuck yourself,* even better. I should be thinking about that miserable car ride home after he'd sent me away. The way I'd fought tears because he'd rejected me so coldly.

"Didn't you like it when I touched you before?" the demon purred.

My whole body stiffened. "Whatever your game is, I'm not playing."

"Game?"

"I don't need your pity fuck."

A long finger curled around my chin turning my head until I stared into those fathomless black depths. "Witchling, whatever are you on about?"

"You shut me down the last time. Hard. I'm not some toy for your amusement."

His brows drew together. "Bella Sanders, do you truly believe I don't want you?" He moved against me, illustrating his point.

"Then why?"

"You were raped, witchling," he said softly. "I've wanted you since the night you summoned me, but I wanted to go slow. To give you time."

Confusion swamped me. He couldn't mean that he'd stopped... for me?

His thumb skimmed along my cheekbone in a gentle caress. "Rest assured, there is no lack of desire on my part, Bella Sanders. We'd only bargained for so much and I was in no state to renegotiate." The corner of his lips curled up into that devilish smile.

MY HEART POUNDED and I was having difficulty swallowing. "You mean that? You really want me?"

In answer, he curved his body over me and brushed his lips lightly across mine. It was a sweeter, more tender caress than I'd ever expected from a demon. He pulled back and looked down at me, waiting.

Stop this, my inner voice shrieked.

Instead, the words, "What will you bargain for it?" escaped.

Declan stilled, dark gaze searching my face. I waited, sinking deeper into his warmth, telling myself that it wouldn't be so bad, that I should do this. It had been over a year since I'd had sex. Despite my better judgment, I was attracted to the demon. Why not use that and get my leverage back?

He was still for so long that I didn't think he was going to answer. Then, "Same deal as last time. An open-ended favor."

My heart thundered in my ribcage. Slowly, so slowly I

rolled in his arms until I pressed fully into him. "It's a bargain."

"A bargain well struck." The way the fire flared in his eyes was the only warning before his lips descended on mine once more. They were soft, especially in contrast to the coarse stubble that coated his chin. And his taste... wicked. Sinful. Hot. Everything that kissing a demon ought to be.

He stroked his tongue between my parted lips. I opened, eager and ready for him. I moaned into his mouth, reveling in the sensation. So many months of build-up, of yearning for his exquisite taste, the feel of his skin against mine.

His hands caressed the length of my body from shoulder to hip and then back again as though he were mapping my flesh. I writhed beneath him. Clothing scattered. His thumb grazed a nipple. I gasped as a jolt of pleasure arrowed down to my lower belly.

He moved back, his burning eyes devouring me as I lay sprawled beneath him like an offering.

"More," I hissed and reached to pull him down where I wanted him.

He groaned before he sucked that tight peak between his lips. This time I didn't hesitate to explore his form. Declan was perfect. Not a scar marred his flesh. Shoulders that he hid in well-tailored suits, were ideal to dig my nails into. His back flexed as he rolled me flat onto mine. I explored the way his muscles bunched and tensed while he shifted to my other side.

I was so lost in his hot kisses and teasing caresses that I didn't realize he'd been pulling down my underwear until he lifted one leg, then the other, leaving me naked except for my socks.

My knees pressed together. I was having trouble catching my breath. Something was happening in my head and my body was just catching up. A sour note spoiled pleasure like lemon juice on a pizza.

Shrewd observer that he was Declan paused, his breaths coming in uneven pants. "Are you all right?"

Sure, other than the fact that I couldn't seem to catch my breath, that adrenaline polluted my bloodstream, and I was fighting tears. Just peachy keen.

His thumb traced my lower lip. "We can stop."

I shook my head, feeling frantic. "The bargain—"

"To hell with the bargain," he snapped.

That put a pause on the low level of unease. I studied his face, the way his jaw clenched, and his gaze burned through me as though it could see past all the outer layers and into the core of me. "You mean that," I whispered.

He nodded and then pressed into me. "I do."

It felt shitty to ask. To stop on the verge. Even I wasn't immune to the whispered words about women who changed their minds halfway through sex. Like we were pulling some sort of bait and switch. Being a tease. I should let him go.

"Would you keep holding me?" I whispered my request, sure he wouldn't. That he'd let me go, say something about needing a minute.

Instead, he collected the loose clothes and reestablished the makeshift blanket. He pulled me close to his side so our bodies were pressed together. He didn't ask for anything, demanded nothing. If I didn't know better I'd think the demon was content just holding me.

~

I WOKE FEELING relaxed once more. Beside me, the demon was snoring.

Freaking adorable. Maybe because everything else about him was so polished and perfect and snoring just didn't fit the image. I studied him as he lay in repose for a long minute.

Maybe we could try again.

The thought whispered in my head. I wanted to, badly. Not just to see if I would make it over the finish line but because I wanted him. Declan. My demon.

What if you can't? Was it fair to get him all worked up again and then ask him to stop? It seemed cruel. I wondered how many times the demon had had sex. Probably every night since I'd summoned him. He'd been free to and between his money and good looks, any number of women and men would have been throwing themselves at him.

And why did that thought sting like salt in a fresh wound?

Shoving my irrational jealousy aside, I pressed my lips into his pectoral, just below a dusky nipple. The snoring cut off abruptly, but he didn't stir. Emboldened, I kissed him again, a little farther down. My fingers explored the terrain. The demon had an eight-pack. Talk about washboard abs. I kissed and licked and reveled in the feel of him, especially when I felt his shaft rising, pressing into my chest.

Surprise surprise, the demon went commando.

Could I be bold? The way I'd been before...everything had changed? Before I'd changed?

"What are you doing, witchling?"

I glanced up to see his eyes were open, those flames dancing.

"Exploring. Can I continue?"

He nodded, wordlessly. I slithered farther down to study his shaft. Thick as my wrist and the tip beaded with seed. Before I could think better of it my tongue flicked over the crown and daubed that little drop away.

"Bella." His fingers speared through my hair. Not demanding or insisting I continue. Just as if he needed another point of contact. Between that and the rasp in his voice when he said my name, he made me crave a deeper taste.

I nuzzled the crisp hairs at his groin and placed soft, teasing kisses along the rigid flesh, even the dusky twin weights below. He shifted and arched and took in a great lungful of air but didn't demand, didn't push me to go any farther or faster. I wondered what it would take to make him beg.

"Witchling," he breathed when I licked up one side of him and down the other like an ice cream cone. "You're killing me."

"You want more?" I asked and proceeded to suckle the head.

"Please," he gasped.

Close enough to begging. I took him deeper. My lips

stretched around him, and I was careful to start slow. To bob up and then glide back down. He made a strangled sound and the hands in my hair tightened as I sucked him inside the hot, wet cavern of my mouth, until the crown hit the back of his throat.

Giving head had never turned me on before. There was something primal about doing it with Declan. The smell of him invaded my senses, his unguarded responses turned me on and made me wet between my legs. I wanted to touch myself there, to come while I made him do the same. I wanted it so I did it. Let my hand slide down to touch myself. I hadn't done it since...

I let that thought go. Just trapped it in a bubble and let it float away. The demon deserved my full, undivided attention.

"Gods above, Bella," Declan bucked as he caught sight of what I was doing. "Does this turn you on?"

I moaned in answer.

"Let me see," he rasped.

I released him and brought the hand I'd been using to stroke myself up between us. He caught my wrist. I started as he took my index finger between his lips.

The flames in his irises shifted to white.

"More," he growled.

Before I knew what was happening, he had moved me onto my back and was spreading my thighs wide, his face inches from my sex.

"You don't—" the protest cut off with a groan as his tongue lashed my clit and then swiped lower.

I arched up off the makeshift bedding. So much feeling. So much pleasure. I would never get enough of him.

My wicked, wicked demon and his pointed tongue played me like an instrument.

It was my turn to tunnel my fingers through his hair as he lapped at me mercilessly. I grew wetter and wetter under his assault. His arms snaked around my thighs, holding me open for his ministrations. Back and forth, he lashed my clit with the tip of his tongue. I trembled all over, on the verge. His lips closed over it, and he sucked. Hard.

The orgasm crashed into me like an oncoming truck. It stole my breath, otherwise I would have screamed.

My release sent him into a fervor, and he lapped madly at my core, even driving his tongue inside prolonging the release, drawing it out longer than I'd ever experienced before.

"Please," I begged, tugging at his hair, trying to get his attention. "It's too much."

He paused and turned his face away, pressing his lips into the meat of my thigh. I watched as he struggled with composure, as though he were fighting to regain control of himself. To do what I asked. I was content to lie there and let the last little tingles settle back down.

"I'm sorry," he murmured.

Propping myself up on my elbows so I could meet his gaze I asked, "Why?"

"I attacked you." Was he blushing?

A laugh bubbled out of me. "Declan, you didn't. You took control and I liked it. The evidence is all over your chin."

He grinned at me, and it was such a charming look

that it stole my breath. "I like knowing I can satisfy you. It's as addictive as your taste."

Something fluttered in my chest. This demon. I glanced down and saw he was still hard, still ready. I licked my lips and met his gaze once more.

"We don't have to," he whispered.

If there had been any doubt in my mind, that assurance, that he would stop if I said the word, killed it. He wanted me. I wanted him. And maybe, just maybe I did trust him. At least with my body.

I gripped his hair and tugged him up until we were nose to nose.. "Shut up, demon, and make love to me."

His mouth crashed into mine. My taste was still on his lips and somehow, the flavor of the two of us mingled made the kiss even more erotic. My legs split wide around his lower body. He smoothed a hand down my side before reaching to angle his shaft. Then, his hand gripped the back of my thigh, pulling me up to him. Declan pressed into me. I was so wet that he slipped between my folds and then drove deep into my core. My body yielded to him completely. If the memories tried to intrude they were burned away in the white-hot heat of his gaze. He surged deep within me, stroking, and caressing spots that I hadn't even known existed.

Not until him.

My nails sank into his back. I stared up into that burning gaze, lost in him and the way he made me feel until it happened again. Another release. My inner muscles clamped around him and coaxed him over the edge. He threw back his head and followed me down into oblivion.

Declan collapsed on his side and rolled me on top of him. He was right, I felt infinitely warmer than I had before. Demon seed, who knew?

"That was better than I could have fathomed," Declan murmured as he stroked my hair away from my face.

"You imagined being with me?" Why did that thought make me grin?

His answer though, made the smile fall right off my face. "With anyone."

Wait.... he wasn't saying. Was he?

When I propped myself up to meet his gaze, he flashed me that charming smile once more. "Don't look so surprised, witchling. I was only born into your world a little over a year ago. There were many other sensations to experience."

"You're a virgin?" I didn't know how to feel about that information.

He shrugged. "Not anymore. Go to sleep."

Did it even matter? We were trapped in hell. "As long as you stop snoring."

He glared up at me. "I do not snore."

My lips curled up in a satisfied smile as I nestled down on his chest. "Go to sleep, demon."

CHAPTER 14
DONNA

It was warmer on the ledge than I would have thought. Maybe because there was no wind. The whole place was like a maze of caverns. My demon guide didn't talk. Exhaustion from the day dragged me into a deep, dreamless sleep.

By the time I woke, disoriented, the demon had vanished. I sat up and scanned the area, hunting for any signs of my guide. Was it daytime? There were no sounds from the Bane, no crashing or screeching.

Could I find my way back to the spring from here? I must. Declan and Bella had been dangerously low on water when I'd left. Once I refilled the canteen we'd have to find a portal. I wished I'd asked my guide where one might be. Funny, demon or not, I'd wanted to know more about the creature who'd saved me more than once yesterday.

I had the odd feeling that if things had been different we might have been...friends

One visit to the demonic plane and my eyes had been

opened. I was beginning to see what a disservice the magic council had done to these beings. This place wasn't just a prison. The hell-realm tortured them, stole their lives bit by bit. Did any living being have the right to consign another to such a fate?

And thinking along those lines I had to admit something else to myself. I'd killed them. Sure, it had been my comeuppance that had lashed out, but I had set it loose. Declan had said it burned. I'd never felt bad about using my power before. Hell, most of the time I was just glad I'd manifested a power at all. I was a Sanders, a legacy witch, but that didn't mean I had all the answers.

When I'd married Lewis, after years of feeling like the broken dud in the Sanders family line, the realization had hit me. *It doesn't have to be this way.* I recalled the first time I'd been diagnosed with ADHD. The bone-deep understanding had flitted through my wonky brain loud as an angel's trumpet. *It doesn't have to be this way.*

The same thought plagued me after all I'd seen. Bella's sacrifice. Declan's fear. My guide's featureless face. The Bane.

It doesn't have to be this way.

But seriously, what was I going to do, set all the demons loose on the mortal plane? Even if I found a way to open a portal and could get them all together, the result would be pure chaos. And maybe some of the demons were happy here?

Okay, slow your roll, Donna. You're getting ahead of yourself. Step one, pee. Step two, try and climb down the noodle tree before you mount an insurrection.

Step one completed, I assessed my physical condition

as well as that of my clothes and boots. There was a hole in the sole of my left boot, an acid burn from where I'd pressed into the sap. I walked in a slow circle, feeling my gait was off, but not enough to leave the protection of my shoes behind. No wonder the demon had been dressed in rags. The hell plane did a number on the wardrobe.

I scraped my hair up into a ponytail and then donned my sock gloves. I'd just shimmied over the edge of the stone precipice when a familiar voice called out, "I was wondering when you'd wake. Hurry up. We're congregating at the meeting house."

I glanced over my shoulder at the demon who looked as bland as banana pudding. "There's a meeting house?" Declan had never mentioned that, only the fighting pits and portals.

When my guide merely stood with hands on skinny hips, I focused on climbing down. The descent felt more treacherous than going up and I was glad at least that I wasn't evading the Bane this time.

"You must be hungry. Here," the demon extended a hand in offering. I blinked. The object was so out of place in the harsh landscape that I experienced a moment of culture shock. "That's an Oreo."

"It's food," the demon insisted. I took the sandwich cookie and turned it around and around, assuring myself it was real. Sure enough, the letters O, R, E, and O were etched into the sides of the chocolate. How had it gotten here? Was someone sending care packages through the portals?

"Where did you get this?" I asked.

"At the meeting house. And if you don't eat it, I will."

Though part of me wanted to pocket it for Bella, the demon's milky eyes watched me too closely. So, I did what I'd been doing for as long as I could remember. Twisted the top and ate the side without the cream first. The sweetness exploded on my tongue and my mouth watered. It had been years since I'd bought Oreos and after days of surviving on carefully rationed protein bars, it was a slice of heaven in the pit of hell.

"How far away is this meeting house?" I asked as the two of us set off in the direction the Bane had come the night before.

"Not far." The day before I'd gleaned that the demon wasn't a big talker and didn't appreciate me peppering questions into our hike. Once we'd left the acidic noodle trees behind, I was happy to follow in its wake. No landmarks, no signs showing this way to the water, that way to certain doom, this way to the portals to get the hell out of here.

"Did you leave anyone behind?" the demon asked me suddenly.

"Yes," I answered honestly. "My son. He wasn't well."

"I think I had a child once." The demon sent me an unreadable glance. "When I see young ones, there's a pang, here." Long slim fingers covered its chest. "I don't know what else it could be."

I wanted to weep. "I'm sorry."

The demon shrugged. "Can you miss what you can't remember? Maybe what you never had?"

I thought about the power that had taken so long to manifest. The well of love I'd practically drowned my son in because I'd had no one else to give it to. That was before. Now I had my sister, her twins, and Axel as well as Devon. My world had expanded, and it had both nothing and everything to do with magic. If I never saw any of them again, if this place eroded my memories, would the ache ever go away?

"Yes," I murmured. "I believe you can."

The demon shot me a tight-lipped smile. "You're all right, Newling. I'm glad you're still alive."

"THAT'S YOUR MEETING HOUSE?" My palms had begun to sweat as we approached. Was my wonky brain playing tricks on me? It couldn't be the Bradbury farmhouse.

Yet it looked eerily like the place where I'd been tortured. The siding was warped, and the entire structure listed to one side, probably because there was no foundation. But the black shutters, the wrap-around porch with peeling paint that I'd crawled across, bloody and broken, all were exactly as I'd remembered.

The shiver that went down my spine had nothing to do with the endless cold.

I wanted to run screaming back to the noodle forest. I wanted to find my sister and shake the hell out of her until answers fell out. How had the farmhouse landed here?

I'd been too battered both in body and spirit to ask too many questions about how Bella and Axel had bested the Servitor. I'd assumed it had something to do with the demon, and that the bargain Bella had made that gave

143

Declan possession of Storm Grove had something to do with it. But I hadn't delved.

Did they know it was here, in the demon under-world? No, I decided. Declan would have warned me. At least I thought he would have.

My guide strode up the rickety steps and held open the screen door. "Come on, Newling."

Heart in my throat I put one foot in front of the other. *She's dead,* I told myself over and over. *Vera Bradbury is dead.*

It didn't help one bit.

The inside of the house was little warmer than the outside. It wasn't the wind that carried a chill in this realm, but the stone itself. Old, rotted timber and tattered insulation did nothing to help buffer the frigid outdoors.

I spied humped figures lying just inside the door beneath blankets and quilts, jackets and clothes. My guide strode past them, toward the kitchen, to where a pack of Oreos sat as though in welcome. The demon plucked one up and made the same twisting motion I had earlier.

I wanted to barf up the cookie I'd eaten. I'd rather starve than subsist out of Vera Bradburry's pantry. My stomach rumbled, betraying the lie.

"Get up, all." My guide called into the other room. "We've got fresh meat."

For a moment I worried that the demon meant that literally. But as more faces appeared from beneath the bedding and nodded at me, I relaxed.

"Newling, meet the crew. Crew, this is Newling," My guide gestured around.

Unsure of what to do I raised a hand in greeting. These demons didn't look at all like the bloodthirsty hoard I'd released Comeuppance upon. Instead, they looked like refugees.

"You're the first we've had in a while," my guide said. "Since years before the conflagration."

"You mentioned that before. What's the conflagration?"

One of the smaller demons perched on the counter-top. It's long skinny legs dangling. "It was when my pa was killed. And all the other warriors in the arena."

Dread pooled in my stomach. It could be a coinci-dence. Somehow I doubted I was that lucky. "Do you know what caused it?"

The young demon shook its head. "No. But the wraiths have been gone ever since. No action at the portals, either. And no one has been summoned."

"Where are the portals?" Hope bloomed in my chest. "Are they nearby?"

My guide chuckled. "So eager to throw your life away, Newling. Do you have any idea what the kinds of witches who summon us are? What do they want us for? Blood and death."

That's not true. I wanted to scream the words. But it would have been a lie. Bella had summoned Declan for revenge. And I doubted any of the witches who did bother with demons had pure motives.

I was fumbling for something to say when the screen door opened once more. A demon wearing a hooded cloak stepped inside. It stopped dead in its tracks when it saw me.

"Donna?"

I started. Unlike the others, this demon was visibly male with broad shoulders and large hands that led to forearms coated with brown hair. Those hands reached up to push the hood away from his face.

My jaw dropped. He looked like a more mature version of Devon.

He had a scruffy beard with red-gold highlights and warm brown eyes that had only slightly begun to lose their pigment.

I shut my mouth and took a step forward. "How do you know who I am?"

He didn't take his gaze from me as he murmured. "Because I'm your father."

CHAPTER 15
BELLA

"Time to get up, witchling."

I groaned and burrowed tighter against the demon's naked body. "I feel like I just fell asleep."

His fingertips followed the bumps on my spine. "You did. But your sister should have been back hours ago. We need to go find her."

That broke my comfy post-coital bubble. "Do you think she's all right?"

He didn't look at me as he reached for his leather pants. "I'm sure she's fine. Probably just lost."

Something about his tone of voice bothered me. "You're lying."

He glanced at me over one shoulder. The flame in his eyes had simmered to a low flicker. "Always believing the best of me."

Did he sound hurt? I ignored it and reached for my clothes. "I'm stressed. Donna's been known to get lost in Shadow Cove, a small town where she's lived her entire

147

life. She doesn't stand much of a chance in the demonic underworld by herself."

He nodded and we continued to dress in silence. I wanted to grasp his hand and thread my fingers through it. Wanted to cling to him to reassure myself that what had happened between us wasn't part of some fantasy. But he seemed so aloof. Stand-offish.

It reminded me of the night I'd summoned him.

The spell had been in our family grimoire, in my mother's neat, precise handwriting. I had wondered why it was there if, as Grand said, only witches who played too close to the line summoned demons. But at the time, lost in despair, I'd just been glad it had been there.

I lit the five candles, drew a circle with salt and called the winds. The only difference was that when I'd utilized the spell in the past, I had stood in the circle. This time the circle stayed empty, a cage for the one whom I summoned.

The Latin chant had been complex, a three out of five on the witchy difficulty scale. I said it three times and then added the name of the demon that had been scrawled beside the spell.

"Asmodeus, I summon thee."

I didn't breathe as I waited. At first, I thought it had failed. That the spell was a joke or maybe some sort of test Mom or Grand had concocted.

Then I smelled it. Brimstone. The cold seeped into my workroom. Two of the candles blew out as a dark fog rolled through the space, gathering into the circle like iron filings to a powerful magnet. A wall of green flames erupted in the center of the circle. I'd thrown my arm up to block the intense white light.

It died as quickly as it came. In the center of my circle stood the most handsome man I'd ever seen.

"You rang, witchling?" The demon crooned. His gaze did a slow perusal of my body and he murmured, "This won't be a hardship at all."

The way he surveyed me with flames in his eyes, that hypnotic croon, the way that he towered over me, all of it made me realize I'd made a mistake.

"Never mind," I tried to smile. "Go on back to your home. I won't bother you again."

He cocked his head to the side, those dark locks seeming to drink in the candlelight. "Pretty little witchling. I sense your pain. Is it vengeance you seek?"

My lips parted. "How did you know?"

"Instinct." The demon smiled. "Boyfriend cheated on you?"

"I wish," the words escaped on an exhale.

The demon studied me for a long moment. It took all my will not to shift under that basilisk gaze. Though I didn't think it was possible, his countenance grew more menacing. Those midnight eyes took in the tear streaks on my face and seemed to read the wound on my very soul.

"Like that, is it? Let me out, witchling. I vow I'll annihilate your enemies. By the time I'm done, there will be nothing left of them but a smear on the ground."

His words made me shiver. I knew he wasn't bluffing. Demons were notoriously ruthless fighters. And yet something stopped me.

His gaze flitted to my abdomen. "Oh, sweet witchling. They have done a number on you, haven't they?"

My breath caught. "How——?"

"Did I know?" More demonic smirking. *"I can read your aura. All of your auras."*

My hand went to my stomach, and I staggered a step. No, it couldn't be.

Except that it could. "Oh, goddess have mercy. what am I going to do?"

It wasn't until his hands closed over my arms that I realized I'd stumbled into my circle, thereby nullifying it. Terror flooded my body as I stared up into those flame-filled eyes. I'd set a demon free. He could shred me to bits. Splatter me on the wall. He could do worse, just as the Bradburys had done.

"Please," I whispered.

"What are you begging for, witchling? A swift end?" The demon crooned.

Slowly I shook my head.

That burning gaze studied my face. "You need to figure out what it is you want. I'll just...go find something to occupy myself until you're ready to make a deal."

He'd eased me to the floor and vanished in a puff of smoke.

I'd passed out and awoken with salt sticking to my cheek and the scent of sulfur burning my nose. I'd run downstairs and out the door, to the drugstore. Three pregnancy tests later, I knew the demon had been correct. I was pregnant.

"Penny for your thoughts, witchling?" Declan touched my arm, causing me to jump.

He looked so different than my memory. Not that he'd changed. He was still beautiful in a dark and foreboding sort of way. He still made my heart race. And the way he'd moved inside me....

Focus, Bella!

"It's nothing," I murmured and then looked around. I didn't smell the sulfur anymore. Was that a bad sign? Dollars to doughnuts we both reeked of it. That and... other things.

"This way," Declan gestured for me to go ahead of him.

"I don't know where I'm going," I pointed out.

"Yes, but we're looking for your twin. You ought to be able to sense her."

"Donna and I aren't like that."

He was watching me closely and I shifted under his scrutiny. "What?"

"You need to listen to your instincts, witchling."

"I do."

One sardonic eyebrow lifted.

"Well, I used to," I corrected.

"What changed?"

"They betrayed me," I muttered.

Declan shook his head. "No, they haven't. You're listening to fear. Not taking risks."

I snorted. "Witches who don't take risks do not wind up in the demonic plane."

He shrugged. "Believe what you will. Close your eyes and think about your sister."

I let out an impatient breath and did as he bade me.

"Feel her energy. How the air in a room changes when she enters it," Declan murmured.

I was having a tough time concentrating on Donna with him standing so close. His energy washed over me, reminding me of what it had been like when he'd spread my legs and surged inside me...

"Focus Bella," Declan muttered.

I blushed. Did he somehow know what I'd been thinking?

As though he really could read my mind Declan muttered, "I can see your aura, remember? Right now, it's a brilliant scarlet color. Not a sign of sisterly affection."

The blush grew deeper. "Sorry."

"Concentrate," he whispered. "Think about Donna."

I thought about Donna. The feeling of her sitting next to me in the doctor's office as the physician spoke the diagnosis. The feel of her in her little car as she drove us to the well. The sound of her voice as she'd tried to call me forth from my nightmare punishment.

It was there, faint, ephemeral, but still a connection. Without opening my eyes, my feet pivoted toward the feeling. I took one step. Then another. And another.

"That's it," Declan said. "Follow your instincts."

I did. Maybe this time they'd save me.

～

Donna

"MY FATHER?" Why did I keep looking for anything to make sense in my life? I was a middle-aged witch who'd reincarnated with her fury lover and was trapped in the demonic plane speaking to her long-lost father. Was this realm fucking with me now? Was that part of the break-you-down strategy, like a mystical boot camp?

We stared at each other for an endless moment. He

really did look like my son. He even had the same freckle beneath his right eye. "Okay, sure, I'll play. What's your name?"

"I don't have one any longer."

"Riiiiiggghhhttt," I raised my brows.

"It's true," he sounded earnest, though lunatics often did. "I traded it for a chance to escape. A summoning name."

"And what happened to that one?" I folded my arms over my chest, as much to retain warmth as to show skepticism.

He frowned. "I don't remember."

I let out an impatient sigh. "You're saying you don't know who you are but somehow you know who I am?"

"It's true, Newling," my guide demon said. "All these little bits of us feed the realm. It's always hungry and we're all it's got. We don't get to select which parts we keep, and which ones are taken from us. Unless we have a piece of shadow stone to preserve the memory."

The newcomer unfastened his cloak and draped it over the counter. When he turned back toward me I spied the same glowing green stone Declan wore.

"This is my most cherished bargain," he said. "The one I made with your mother."

I wanted to shout that there was no way that my father was a demon. But that was both foolish and possibly deadly. Hadn't I been coming around to their plight? Understanding the evils of this place and what it took for them to survive?

"So, you know my mother," I asked Demon-Dad.

He nodded. "I was summoned by her to continue her line."

I held up both hands. "Her line? You're talking about the Sanders line of witches?"

He nodded eagerly.

I began pacing the length of the floor. My mind had been bent into a pretzel. I didn't know up from down. Bella had lied to me, kept things from me. And now...him.

We didn't know who our father had been. Dads weren't recorded in the family grimoire. I'd asked Mom once and she'd look so sad that I'd never asked again.

That's the way it was with Sanders legacy witches. No fathers. Only moms and twins as far back as our recorded history went. All the way back to Edith Sanders whose husband had died in a mysterious accident.

"Generation after generation of twins. Always twin girls," I murmured. At least up until us,

"The name went with the family. To be summoned by a Sanders witch was the best a demon could hope for," Demon-Dad said.

The name went with the family. The room spun. A chair sat beside the kitchen table. I sank heavily onto it. "Asmodeus," I breathed.

"That was it!" Demon-Dad looked pleased as punch, as though I'd given him a great gift.

I hung my head. Bella had said she found the summoning spell in the family grimoire, complete with the name. But if the name was what the demons fought over, what they were vying for was the chance to impregnate one of us.

Until Bella had broken the cycle. Because Declan held the name and she'd already been pregnant.

"Why did we not know this?" I whispered. "Someone should have told us what was going on."

"Demonic blood is potent," Guide-demon said. "And being summoned to have a child with a witch is the only way we can procreate."

Again, that long limbed hand hovered over the demon's midsection. As though cradling a phantom child.

My mind whirled under the weight of these revelations. I'd believed the banishment had been rough. Never mind that these magical prisoners had been used for breeding stock.

"So why did Mom sacrifice herself to keep the portal closed?" I asked.

Dad demon looked sad. "That wasn't her intention. She was trying to find a way to recover me. To let me out and enjoy a mortal life with her. And with you girls. I wanted that more than anything."

I believed him. As crazy as the whole thing sounded, I bought it, hook, line, and sinker. I'd always wanted a dad. Who cared that he was a demon? Well, I was sure the other witches would care but they could go fuck themselves.

"Okay, so, Demon-Dad," I addressed him, and he flashed me Devon's grin. Eerie. Blood didn't lie, there was a relation there. "I need you to help us find a portal."

"Us?" he asked.

"Bella's here too, along with her...friend."

"Oh no." Dad frowned. "Then who will open the portal?"

"Axel, I hope," I said. "He's my, uh...guy."

"Oh, is that the fury?" Dad asked.

I blinked. "You know him too?"

"Only by reputation. The wraiths whispered about the newcomer to Storm Grove and his uncanny abilities. I knew a fury once...." He stared out into the ether, then shook his head. "At least I think I did."

Poor Demon-Dad was hopelessly muddled. I laid a hand on his arm. "The portal?"

He blinked and then looked back at me. "Oh, sure. Are we going to find Bella now?"

I put a hand on his arm. "Yes and boy, are we going to have a whole lot of catching up to do."

CHAPTER 16
BELLA

"I'm going to kill her," I grumbled.

We'd been walking for what felt like endless hours. Donna's trail had led us first to a cavern that Declan had refused to let me go inside because it "reeked of toxins." No Donna. Then we'd come across a spring followed by a forest that looked as though it had been cooked *al dente*. No Donna.

"Where the hell is she?" I stopped in the middle of a corridor that looked like so many others.

"Easy witchling," the demon soothed.

I shot him a glare and murmured, "She knows better than to go exploring on her own."

She shouldn't have left in the first place, but I wasn't about to blame the demon for that. Donna saw a problem, namely our shortage of water, and she'd been determined to fix it. That was my sister in a nutshell—a fixer.

"We'll find her." Declan made the same soothing sounds he'd made when I'd cried after awakening in the demonic realm.

"Damn it, what if she needs help? What if she's bumbling around in this labyrinth trying to find her way back? Donna gets lost in Shadow Cove."

A hand landed on my shoulder. I paused mid-tirade, basking in his warmth, and met his burning gaze. "Trust that whatever she's doing, it's for a good reason."

"That's easy for you to say," I griped. "It's not your sister that's MIA, demon."

His hand fell away, and he glared at me. "Do you have something to say? Spit it out before you choke, Bella."

What was his damage? "It seems like you're the one having a fit. You've been running hot and cold all day."

"And there it is." He shut his eyes again and leaned his head against the wall of pulsing green stone.

His words made me feel hollow inside. "There what is?"

"Nothing."

I was about to make a snide comment when I got a good look at him. His skin appeared almost sickly in the glowing light of the rock, his hair was disheveled because he'd been running his hands through it. Over the past two days, his beard stubble had grown in, giving him a scruffy appearance, I'd never seen on him before. He seemed...broken.

"Are you all right?" I whispered.

He laughed and it wasn't a pleasant sound. When his eyes opened the fire within flickered and danced. "Do you care?"

I bristled. "Of course, I care."

"Then tell me, witchling, what are we?"

What? "You're jonesing for a relationship label *now*?"

"Humor me."

I didn't know how to qualify our relationship. Were we friends? Lovers? Summoner and

sommonee? I thought of the way he held my children. How we'd danced together at the gala. How he touched me last night, the way his eyes had burned as we'd made love. Unnerved, I whispered, "What do you want me to say? I care about you. Isn't that enough for now?"

He cocked one jet eyebrow. "Seems to me, witchling, that the only person you care about is yourself."

I reared back as though he'd slapped me.

Declan shook his head. "The more I see of your world, the greed, the corruption, the more I realize that at least here, demons are honest about their intentions to use one another. We're all fighting for survival. What's your excuse?"

I glared at him, insulted. "I don't use people."

He laughed again. "The only reason you summoned me was for revenge. I was a tool to you and have been ever since I stepped foot outside your little protection circle."

My lips parted. What was I supposed to say? I had summoned a demon to kill the Bradburys after what they'd done to me. "I thought we'd come to an understanding about that."

"No, what we came to was an agreement. Another fucking bargain. If I want anything from you, I must barter for it because that's the only way you'll interact with me at all. When you want something!"

His words hurt and I lashed out with reflection. "Me? What about you? Building your little empire. You think I don't know what you're doing?"

He cast me a wary look and I felt sure he could see himself in my gaze "I don't know what you're talking about."

I poked him in the chest. The air grew colder, and my teeth chattered as I spat the words. "You may have left this place but at the end of the day, you're still fighting to escape the arena and build something that no one can take away from you. Guess the fuck what? Life doesn't work that way! It doesn't matter how much money you have stashed in your underwear drawer or how many hotels you own. There's nothing that you can hold onto forever, Asmodeus, not one damned thing in this entire miserable universe."

"Do. Not. Call. Me. That!" he snarled.

"Why not? Isn't that the name you fought for? The one that set you free?"

I don't know if it was the use of his summoning name or just that I'd got his temper up, but he lunged across the small space that separated us until he hovered over me. His hands gripped my upper arms. I swayed, wanting to lean into his heat. He was the only source of warmth in this goddess-forsaken place. But I still kept a shred of pride.

Through gritted teeth, he snapped, "Because every time you do, it reminds me what I am. And what we can never be."

The hurt on his face snapped me out of my rage. "I don't understand."

"Tell her." A voice said from off to our left. "It's time someone started owning their shit."

"Donna!" I shoved past Declan but stopped when I saw the bearded man beside her. "Who's that?"

My sister looked the worse for wear. Her hair was disheveled, and she had dirt beneath her fingernails. Her clothes were torn, and she appeared to be limping slightly.

But her eyes were the worst of all. "Bella," she breathed. "This is our father, Asmodeus."

"What?" She must be hallucinating. Like the people in Shadow Cove, the seep of the underworld had gotten to her. "Donna, this is Asmodeus." I gestured to Declan. "You know that."

I chanced a glance up at Declan, whose face had gone pale as he stared at the other man.

I looked from him to the stranger to Donna. "This doesn't make any sense. What's she talking about, Declan?"

"I took it from you," Declan whispered, his gaze still on the bearded man. "The summoning name."

The man frowned as though he were trying to concentrate and then breathed, "Yes. I remember now. I didn't want it anymore. Not after she died."

"She being Mom," Donna said. "The demons verified it. They all told me that being summoned by a Sanders witch was an honor. Because our foremothers have been using demons as studs to ensure a strong magical line. All the way back to Edith."

It couldn't be. I stared up at Declan, willing him to deny it. What I saw there chilled me even more than the ever-present cold. If he'd looked pale before, now his face was ashen. The flames in his midnight eyes burned bright with visible fear.

"It can't be true," I whispered.

He shook his head. "It wasn't supposed to go this way. You were supposed to know how it worked."

"Well, I didn't!" I hissed. "And I guess you couldn't be bothered to explain it to me?"

He reached for me. "Witchling—,"

"Do not call me that." I wrenched out of his grasp and stumbled closer to Donna. Her expression had softened somewhat, but she still looked half a heartbeat away from rabid.

"I trusted you," I breathed. "I knew better. Damn it, I knew it was stupid. That I couldn't count on you."

He flinched and took a hesitant step toward me.

"Get away from me," I snapped. "I never want to see you again."

"You don't mean that." His gaze traveled down my body, to my stomach.

No. No no *no*. It was just once. I couldn't be pregnant. Not so soon. I was still nursing, which lowered the risk of pregnancy.

But there had been no milk. Not since that first night after the gala when he'd...

"Did you do something to me?" I whispered. "To stop my milk?"

"No," he shook his head vehemently. "Bella, I wouldn't do that."

"I don't believe you." I was going to vomit. Right there on the throbbing green floor. He'd planned this.

Planned to knock me up. He didn't care that I already had twins. He wanted his own. Hell, he'd made me believe the sex had been my idea.

That look he'd had on his face all day, that I'd been concerned over? That was guilt. Because he'd duped me.

It was only once! My mind screamed. But I knew better than anyone, that once was all it took. And Declan could read auras.

"Bella, please." The demon reached for me again.

I called my magic and held witchfire, the sort that would burn through anything. Stone or flesh or bone, witchfire ate it all. He eyed the brilliant flame warily and then raised both hands and took a step back. "Don't use magic here. You know the price."

"I don't care." I lifted my chin, letting my power flow through me, "So help me, if I ever catch a glimpse of you again, I will burn you to ash."

The fire in his eyes dimmed. He nodded once then dissolved into smoke.

And I fell to the floor, my face in my hands, and sobbed.

~

Donna

I DIDN'T KNOW how much more my sister could take. She looked as though the news about the demon had just gutted her. Maybe it had. Maybe I shouldn't have told her. But I was in over my head and sick to death of being lied to.

"Bella, get up." I snapped.

She shook her head.

"Bella, tell me why the fricking Bradbury farmhouse is in the fricking demon realm."

That got her attention. Slowly, her hands lowered to her knees, and she looked up at me. "What?"

"The farmhouse where I was tortured? It's here. Did you have something to do with it?"

Don't lie to me, I silently begged her. *Do not fucking lie to me again.* Anything else we could come back from but not if she lied to my face.

She swallowed and bobbed her head.

I shut my eyes and whispered, "How? No witch spell can transport something so large to another realm. How did you do it?"

She swallowed visibly. "Demon magic."

My lids popped open, and I stared down at her. "Are you fucking kidding me with this?"

"It was the only way," she protested. "The only way to get the Servitor out of our world." Her eyes went wide with fright. "Is it here too?"

I turned to Demon-Dad. "Have you seen a big flying menace around here? Not the Bane. This creature is different."

His brows drew together. "I don't think so."

Neither did I. The servitor had a way of making itself known.

"So, you fucked around with demon magic. Let me guess, what caused the rift? That was why you had to be the one to heal it?"

She nodded miserably and whispered, "I'm sorry."

Disgusted, I paced in a circle.

Demon-Dad crouched beside Bella. "It's okay. We all make mistakes."

"Some more than others," I said tartly.

Bella was staring at him. He offered her a hand. "Bella. I'm so thrilled to finally meet you."

She took his hand and let him pull her to her feet. Her gaze searched his features. "He looks like Devon."

"I'm pretty sure Devon looks like him," I corrected.

Bella swallowed. "Asmodeus, the demon of lust. It's a title."

"Yes," Demon-Dad said. "The most coveted one. The Sanders witches are reputed to be kind. No beatings, no chains. A demon who is summoned by them is treated well until the bargain is complete."

"And then?" Bella asked. "What happens after the bargain is over?"

"We're sent back here." He smiled sadly. "Your mother tried to come after me. She wanted it to stop. Wanted to free the demons. But the portal was too heavily guarded. The demons at the gate were infuriated that a witch would come through. They tore her apart." A tear dripped down his cheek.

Bella staggered and I steadied her even as I asked, "Are those demons still nearby?"

He shook his head. "No. The conflagration wiped them all out."

"What?" Bella asked.

"I'm pretty sure that's what the demons call the night the portal was sealed. When the twins were born." I cast her a meaningful glance. She knew what had happened, what I'd done, unleashing comeuppance.

Her green eyes went wide. "Oh."

"Most of the demons are dead now," Demon-Dad said. "A few of us have been hiding and struggling to survive ever since. With fewer of us to feed on, the realm takes more and more each time we wield."

I met Bella's gaze. "We can't leave them here to be broken down like cars being stripped for parts."

My sister looked like she might vomit. Was she thinking about using demonic magic? That if any other witch found out they would consign her to the same fate?

"But we can't just set the whole demon population loose on Shadow Cove? Haven't I done enough damage?"

She was talking about the rift. The hallucinations.

"Bella," I put a hand on her arm. "We can't leave them here to die. That's what the Magic Council did. And while I get that you are super pissed at Declan, consider why he did what he did. For survival. Bella, this is what Mom wanted to do. Don't we owe it to her, to them, to set them free?"

My sister stared at me for a long moment. "How?"

I swallowed and then looked at Demon-Dad. "You said you could take us to the portal?"

When he nodded I breathed, "Then, let's go."

As we walked, Bella slipped her hand into mine. "Donna," I'm so sorry."

"You should have told me." It was a familiar refrain. Bella decided and she believed was for the best. I ended up paying the price.

166

She looked so miserable as she whispered, "I know. It's all my fault. The rift, the fact we're stuck here."

"ADHD equals impulse control issues," I told her.

"Tell me about it," she groused.

"But Bella, look at it this way. Maybe we're supposed to be here. To help these demons."

She said nothing.

"They aren't all bad. I think I got the ones who were all bad," I whispered. "The ones without any humanity. But these demons, they're just people. Witches who got caught making a bad call. You can't tell me you don't know what that's like. Imagine being punished for the rest of your life for one lousy choice."

She nodded. "Okay."

I squeezed once. "Do you think you're pregnant?"

She didn't turn a hair. "I could be."

"Do you love him?"

"He's a demon."

"Mom loved a demon," I pointed out. "I love a fury. It's not outside the scope of possibility."

She laughed, but there was no humor in the sound. "Maybe it should be. Maybe Sanders witches aren't meant to love anyone but their children."

I tugged her to a stop. "You're not saying you're okay with the whole demon stud thing?"

She shook her head. "No. What I'm saying is I don't think we're built for long-term relationships. That's why we make such disastrous picks."

I didn't correct her. Mostly because I feared she might be right.

CHAPTER 17
BELLA

The demon arena was nothing like what I'd imagined. The term arena suggested the Colosseum with curved seats rising above the action. Or at least something as impressive as the bleachers that flanked the Shadow Cove High School football field. The demonic arena was nothing but an open area with more of the same oozing green stalactites. Any spectators would have been in the line of fire. I saw Donna wince at the scorch marks and what looked like drops of blood that stained the glowing green stone. Her comeuppance had caused the annihilation of the demons who'd been congregated here, and she felt guilty about it.

Never mind that those demons had been the worst of the worst. The ones who'd would have killed Donna if Axel hadn't caught her. Was guilt one of those universal things that applied to everyone? I felt guilty for using demon magic. Hell, for summoning a demon in the first place. Donna felt it because she'd taken out the blood-thirsty hoard in this arena. And Declan....

I shoved all thoughts of him from my mind. If the demon felt guilty for not telling me the truth, then that was his problem.

The portal, for there was only one on this side, swirled overhead. According to Demon-Dad, it didn't open on this side unless someone was being tossed through.

"They always landed right in the arena?" Donna asked.

Demon Dad nodded. "Many of the more bloodthirsty demons would wait here for them. They'd taken the newcomers out as soon as they landed."

"Why?" I whispered, thinking about our poor mother who'd tried to save her lover.

"For retaliation. Some were mad and thrived on violence. The worst of our kind congregated here. And the victors enslaved the losers. If they let them live at all."

And Declan had to beat all of them to acquire a summoning name. *Don't think about him.*

But I was having trouble keeping my thoughts from him. The things he'd said. *She left me when I was barely old enough to crawl. With the rest of the children destined for the demon's fighting arena. You think all demons are created equal? No, dearest witchling, we must carve our places out by defeating those weaker than ourselves. I spent years fighting to attain my rank. Hoping to be awarded a name."*

"You mean your summoning name."

"I mean any name at all, other than slave. And even once you reach the summit, there's always someone trying to knock you down. To take your place."

169

Donna touched my arm. "You okay?"

I shook away the memory. "Fine. What's the game plan?"

"Honestly, there isn't one. I know zilch about portals. And it makes no sense that there are so many on the mortal plane and only the one here."

"They must funnel to this exit," I studied the sealed portal. "Like water from the sink, tub, and toilet in one bathroom all going down the same pipe to the sewer."

"Charming analogy," Donna walked around in a circle. "Okay, so we know this portal is meant to be one way. "If that's the case, why did the wraiths keep trying to open it to let the demons out?"

"Wraiths?" Demon-Dad frowned.

"Spirits that take over mortals," I explained.

"Oh, you mean the disembodied."

Donna and I exchanged a look. "Disembodied?"

"Those that have died a physical death in this place," his lucidity came and went. I wasn't sure where he fell on the spectrum as he spoke.

"So why do all the beings they inhabit keep trying to open the portals on our side?" Donna asked.

He shrugged. "Maybe they just want the witches to see what it was like here."

I swallowed hard. For years it had been my job to guard the portal for fear of a demonic invasion. And in one sentence Demon-Dad was making me reconsider everything.

Suddenly I felt dizzy. "I need to sit."

Donna put an arm around my shoulders and helped me to a nearby rock. "Easy Bella."

I put my head between my knees. "How could they have done it? How could the magic council just send people to this place on a whim?"

"I don't know," my sister rubbed the spot between my shoulder blades. "It's not like they got rid of all the evil witches either. Because the entire Bradbury clan was still able to do damage. It's just the ones who made trouble or drew human attention to themselves."

I took a deep breath. "We need to burn this whole place to the ground."

"How?" Donna asked. "With witchfire?"

I shook my head. "No, it's too big and we'd burn out our magic before we took out a quarter of it. Besides, we need to get out of here before we consider dropping a nuke in behind us."

"Not that we have a nuke," Donna grumbled. She rose and began to pace. "I have an idea. But I'm not sure if I'll be able to reach him."

"Who?"

"Axel." She smiled. "I touched his dreams the other night. I didn't realize it at the time but the memory he was having? I did a spell trying to figure out a way to help him and I ended up in the same place. If I can do it again, maybe I can get him a message."

I nodded. "It's the best we've got. Tell me what you need."

Donna

171

"Half-baked plan, check. Reflective surface, check," I murmured as I stared into the battered shield that Demon Dad had propped up against a glowing green stone. He and Bella had moved off to the far end of the arena so they wouldn't distract me.

I had no candle to burn so I set up a torch made from a discarded spear and lit it using witchfire. The effort made me feel sick to my stomach. The horrible place taking its toll.

I let my gaze go unfocused and chanted the Shadow of Self spell I'd used the other night. *"Lucerna mea prae-teritam aperit."* Candlelight reveals my past.

Lina, I thought. *I'm Lina and he's Gunther.*

I couldn't get too lost in the past life. If I forgot all about where I was and what I needed Axel to do, we were screwed. Lucid dreaming to the max.

Slowly, I rocked back and forth, letting my gaze go unfocused, emptying my mind of all that had come before, all my worries and concerns.

My reflection in the shield wavered and then faded. And the scene unfurled.

Lina and Gunther lying nestled together on a pallet before a roaring fire. They were naked and flushed from lovemaking. With one hand she reached out and touched a stone that hung on a leather cord around his neck. Somehow I knew she'd given that to him. A talisman for good health. She murmured something in German, something I couldn't understand.

I could feel the frustration coming off him, but I didn't think it originated from Gunther. It emanated from a man who was hunting for something but couldn't find it and didn't want to be sidetracked. In my mind I reached out farther, hunting for Axel.

And then suddenly, I was no longer witnessing the scene. It was my body pressed up against his. My mind had taken charge.

Our eyes met and I felt that familiar flutter.

"I need your help," I told him. Lina told him. In English.

His brows drew together and I saw him inhale.

I could even smell you, he'd said.

"Axel," I breathed. "It's me. I need your help."

"Don?" He whispered.

"Yes. We're trapped on the demon plane. I need you to find a way to open the portal."

"The portal?" He frowned. "The one we sealed off?"

I nodded. "It's the straightest shot out of here. Please. Hurry."

With that, the witchfire died and I sat staring at my reflection.

"Did it work?" Bella called out.

I lay back on the ground and stared at the ceiling, willing the portal to open. "I guess we'll find out."

He'd need time to get back to Storm Grove, time to figure out how to reopen what had been sealed. And even if he did, we needed to find a way to reverse the current so that we could leave.

I sat up, decision made. "Gather all the demons that you know of and bring them here."

"What are you thinking?" Bella asked.

"You want to destroy this place? Let's take away its food source."

Bella

"So, we have a dad," Donna said as she plopped down beside me. "How about that?"

"What exactly are we supposed to do with him?" I asked. The demon had promised to go collect the others and bring them to the arena so we would be ready to go if Axel did manage to open the portal.

Donna shrugged. "I don't know. Get to know him I guess."

"How are you taking this so well?" I asked her.

She cast me a sideways glance. "Believe me, I'm not."

I shook my head. "I can't believe what's been going on here. I mean Declan's talked—" I cut myself off.

Donna put a hand on my arm. "It's okay to talk about him, you know."

"No, it isn't." I dropped my head into my hands. "I need to forget about him."

"Does that mean you want to leave him here?" She asked.

Lifting my head, I turned to stare at her. "How can you ask me that?"

"Well, it seems to me that's what witches have been doing for a very long time. Disposing of people who caused them difficulties in this place. Letting it devour them a little bit at a time. Out of sight out of mind. Problem solved."

Tears stung my eyes. "You know I'm not like that."

"What about Mom?" Donna challenged. "What about Grand? Demon-Dad said Mom was searching for a way to free him. That gives me a little comfort. But Grand did a summon hit it and quit it without batting an eye."

"Why do you hate her?" I asked. Grand had taken care of us.

"I don't hate her, Bella. But I see exactly how flawed she was. And as someone different, what with my wonky brain and all, I have a problem with the idea that anyone who doesn't meet an arbitrary standard is disposable." She turned away. "That was why I wanted you to have the diagnosis. I know labels don't matter to you, but I thought you'd get it. That we are different from what's come before. Both of us. You were always this fantastic witch, and I was...I am...a mess."

I swallowed hard. "You're not a mess. You're incredible, Donna. I wish I had half your strength. Or your compassion."

"It's better than being bitter." She sighed. "You know what? I've been worried because of this whole past life connection. That Axel wanted Lina and that I'm not Lina. I thought that when he realized that he wouldn't want me anymore."

"That's crazy," I shook my head.

"Yeah, I know. He kept telling me that I was Lina. And I think I finally figured out what it was he meant. The parts about me that love him, those parts don't have a name or a waistline measurement or ADHD or anything else. Those parts simply exist to love him, you know?"

Tears stung my eyes. I did know.

My sister turned to me and met my gaze. "Do you love him?"

"Are we talking about Axel or Demon-Dad?" I quipped.

Donna bumped my shoulder. "You know who I mean."

I stared off into nothing. "He lied to me."

"No, he withheld shit from you. That's different."

I opened my mouth to argue but Donna cut me off. "Look, Bells. I understand why you're upset. But did you ever consider the fact that we're in this mess because you're too terrified to live?"

"That's not true."

"Really?" Donna challenged. "You did what Grand told you. Never questioned it, just obeyed orders. Upheld the legacy. Even threw me away because you thought I was a dud. You dated Zeke Bradburry, hell you even summoned a demon. But in the end, you're still the legacy witch of Shadow Cove. And you know what, I think you hate it."

A lump formed in my throat, and I couldn't think of a single thing to say.

"When I pretended to be you I got a taste of what it's like. I thought it would be great to have everyone respect me and maybe even be a little afraid of me. But you know what I realized? It's lonely as hell."

"What else am I supposed to be?" I whispered.

"Whatever the hell you want." Donna shrugged. "Maybe a demon's lover. Maybe not. The point is it's time you quit worrying about what all those witches who came before us wanted. Stop fretting over the legacy. Because guess what? All those Sanders witches? They all kinda sucked."

A little laugh bubbled out of me.

"Seriously. They couldn't handle a relationship on their own. Couldn't even manage to bag a Lewis." She crossed her eyes and stuck out her tongue.

"Stop it," I laughed. "I'm going to wet my pants."

"Follow your heart, Bella," Donna sobered and covered my hand with hers. "It's what I plan on doing. If we ever get out of here."

"You'll get out, Donna Sanders-Allen," a familiar voice crooned from behind us.

I stiffened even as Donna rose and dusted off the seat of her jeans. "I'll let you two talk."

"Stay," Declan said. Was he worried I'd toss witchfire at him as I'd promised?

Donna glanced at me as I too got up and turned around.

"What is it?" I asked Declan, glad my voice didn't shake.

"I found a way to reverse the portal once it's been opened on the mortal plane." He held out a scroll to Donna. "But there's a price."

"Isn't there always?" I murmured even as Donna asked, "What price?"

Those dark eyes fixed on my face. "The portal can only be sealed from this side. Otherwise, we're back to where we started with the hallucinations. Someone's got to stay behind."

CHAPTER 18

DONNA

I studied the scroll the demon had unfurled on one of the large boulders. "Where did you get this?"

"It was in the archives," Declan muttered. "I went there to...sort through things."

"Like the fact you went and intentionally knocked my sister up without telling her that was your sole purpose?" Maybe it wasn't fair to blame him. But fuck it, I was in no mood to be fair. Bella had ADHD and twin six-month-olds at home. Should she have used birth control before getting with Declan? Yeah. But he had kept vital information from her. So, I had her back.

"She's not pregnant," the demon muttered, glancing over his shoulder to where Bella stood beneath the portal, drawing the runes on the scroll.

My jaw dropped. "You lied to her? *Again*?"

He shifted, looking uncomfortable. "It's all I know how to do."

"Ugh. You're a dick, you know that? I can't believe I was rooting for you." I shook my head in disgust.

x

That seemed to amuse him. "Were you then?"

"Yes, okay? But that was when I thought you wanted to make her happy."

Declan sobered. "I do."

"Whatever, I'm out." I'd had more than enough drama in the past three days to last me a lifetime. "But if you were playing games, then tell her. And tell her it's because you're a big fat chicken."

"I'm not fat," he blustered.

No denying that he was a chicken though. I decided to rub it in and started clucking at him.

The demon shook his head. "You are one of a kind, Donna Sanders-Allen. No one in history has been so concerned with setting things right with demon kind."

I shrugged. "Honestly? I'm hoping I don't live to regret it."

Declan moved away to converse with Bella, and I refocused on the scroll. The spell itself was simple but required the powers of a legacy witch in the demonic plane to open the gate. Once opened, the portal could be held by one soul, the sacrifice who remained behind and would bear the brunt of the plane's need.

I stood and closed my eyes. In the arena, I could feel the echoes of the demons I'd killed. It ought to be me. Bella had babies and cared for Declan. The two of them should go back.

Could I resign myself to never seeing Axel again? Never hug Devon or finding out what his life would be like? Would he go back to college? Would he think I'd abandoned him?

I didn't want to do it. Didn't want to give up the life

I'd only just begun to piece together. Maybe we were being too hasty. There could be another way.

"Donna!" Demon-Dad raised a hand and came shambling over to where I stood.

Despite my initial reservations, he was growing on me. "Hey, you. You looking forward to seeing the last of this place?"

He nodded and then pulled me into a hug. "I'm proud of you. You and your sister. Your mother would be proud too."

"Thanks." I hugged him back. Funny how strange it had felt only a few hours ago. Now it seemed like the most natural thing in the world.

Just another thing I didn't want to lose.

Bella

"CAN WE SPEAK?" Declan murmured.

"I'm busy." My gaze was intent on the runes I was drawing in the sand. I wanted to get them just right so that the portal would open at Storm Grove. Anywhere else and we'd have a whole lot of trouble explaining the sudden appearance of thirty-plus demons.

"You're not pregnant."

That got my attention. I sat back on my heels and stared up at him. "Another lie?"

"I panicked. Witch—Bella," he corrected. "I didn't want you to send me away before I could explain."

I studied his face and sudden understanding flooded through me. "You're going to stay behind."

He nodded. "I wouldn't have brought the scroll unless I planned to be the one to hold the portal open."

"I can summon you again," I whispered. "Once I get back to Storm Grove."

"Don't do that." There was a catch in his voice as he explained. "I don't think there'll be anything left for you to summon."

I blinked at him. "You're saying this...staying behind is a death sentence?"

He swallowed. "It always was."

"There has to be some other way?" I was shaking my head over and over. "Something else we haven't thought of yet."

His dark eyes were somber. "There is one thing you can do for me. Give me a chance to explain."

I nodded and then cast my gaze toward the door that was packed with demons. "Can we go somewhere else? I'd rather not have an audience."

Though I wasn't about to tell Declan, the demons who'd been broken down by the realm, had their features muted, and the pigment in their eyes and hair faded, freaking me out.

And what do you think is going to happen to Declan after you leave? A snide inner voice hissed.

"The archives are nearby. Let me show you." He offered me a hand and after a moment's hesitation, I took it.

The archives were only a few hundred yards from the arena. A crude roof had been built over the alcove and a tattered piece of fabric hung over the opening. Declan held it aside for me and I passed by him and looked around the eight-by-ten-foot space.

Glowing green orbs, similar to Declan's necklace illuminated the space. Shadow stones. Niches had been carved out of the wall that stretched a hundred feet up and held scrolls. Hundreds and hundreds of them. I'd believed Declan's collection of demon magic was impressive, but it was nothing compared to such a collection.

"Where did all of these come from?" I asked as I surveyed the space.

"No one knows for sure. The realm may provide them, to encourage us to use magic. A way to feed it." He sat down on a low boulder. I got the impression he was doing so intentionally so that he wasn't looking at me. "I used to sleep here, as a boy. About fifty feet up there's an alcove big enough that I fit in."

I tried to imagine scaling that wall up and down every day. "Why?"

He swallowed. "I wasn't faster or stronger than the other demons who fought in the ring. I had to be cleverer. To only utilize magic when I desperately needed it and to know which spells would get me what I wanted. To win the title of Asmodeus."

I stared at him for an endless moment.

"Bella, I'm so sorry. I should have told you everything a long time ago."

"Why didn't you?"

He shrugged. "At first I didn't know you. Didn't trust you. My very presence seemed to

agitate you. Your world was brand new to me. It's....

overwhelming after this. The colors, the choices. I knew things about magic but when it came to being a person, to living an actual life? I was completely unprepared."

"You managed."

He nodded. "I did. But you always had the power to send me back here. You even threatened to do it a couple of times."

I grimaced. "I know. I'm sorry. That was wrong."

"It was," Declan agreed. "But I understand now what you were protecting. Your family, your legacy. I have very few memories of my mother. Astrid and Ember deserve to have more."

A lump formed in my throat. "You won't fight?" *Not even for me?* I wanted to ask but couldn't. It wasn't fair for me to put that sort of pressure on him.

"I'm tired of fighting." He scrubbed a hand over his face. "The desk in my inner sanctum holds the deed to Storm Grove. I've left it to Astrid and Ember."

My lips parted. Before I could say anything, he continued, "The rest of my holdings belong to you. I'd recommend you visit the property on the Outer Banks first. There's a nice little community out there and the witch in charge is worth meeting."

I shook my head. "I don't want it. I don't want any of it."

His gaze had gone unfocused but at my words, he turned to face me. "I wish I had more to give you. I would have liked more time to make you understand what a gift you gave me. I know you regret summoning me. But I never did. Not once, witchling."

My eyes were swimming as I stepped forward. "There has to be another way."

He didn't seem to hear me. "Forgive me for all the games?"

"There's nothing to forgive." Oh goddess, this was really happening. Declan was saying goodbye.

He put a hand to my face and cupped my cheek. "This is what I want to remember to the end. Your face, just as it is now."

I leaned up on my toes and kissed him. It wasn't a gentle kiss. Our mouths crashed together. His heat washed over me even as I gripped the silky dark mass of his hair in my hands. We'd messed up. Wasted the time we'd been given. No longer.

My back hit the wall and I broke the kiss even as I reached for his leather pants. "I want you."

"Bella," he moaned as I cupped him through the leather.

"Call me witchling." Tears tracked from my eyes. I couldn't seem to stop them any more than I could stop the frantic pace of my hands as I shoved fabric out of the way.

That devilish grin appeared, and his eyes filled with fire as he looked at me. "Witchling. My witchling." His index finger slid past my underpants and along the folds of my sex. The touch made me gasp.

"So wet," Declan whispered as that finger breached me. "Goddess, you have no idea how tempting you are to one like me."

"Show me then," I fought my clothes, shoving the pants and underwear down and kicking one leg free, before gripping his length. "Show me how I tempt you."

He gripped me by the back of my thighs and hoisted me up. My back hit the wall and my arms wrapped around his neck. His tongue slid into my mouth as his shaft prodded my core. I wriggled, needing to feel him stretch me, fill me.

"Please," I begged. I didn't care. Any bargain he wanted to make, I'd agree. Just so long as I got to feel all of him, as deep as he could go.

"Slowly, love." He murmured as he inched up inside me. "I want to savor this. To savor you."

My whole body shook as he pressed closer, farther, slowly invading the flesh that gripped him greedily. My eyes fluttered, my thighs clenched as he guided my legs around his waist so he could move even deeper.

His forehead rested against mine when he bottomed out inside me. The orgasm was just there, just out of my reach. I didn't shut my eyes, my gaze locked with his.

He tipped his head down. His lips parted as he watched himself withdraw, just as agonizingly slowly as he'd entered me. Color suffused his cheeks as he watched our joining, seemingly in awe of the way we fit together. My inner muscles clamped down on him again and again. The world beyond us ceased to exist.

"My witchling," he nuzzled my cheek, my ear as he sank inside again. "Will you come for me? Let me feel your pleasure?"

"Declan," I moaned, loving the soft, easy glide, the way my body adjusted to accommodate him. The frenetic need I'd had to have him in me was replaced now with the desire to stretch this out for as long as we possibly could. Forever wouldn't be long enough.

"I've wanted you from the first moment I saw you," he said as he kissed my ear. "I wanted everything from you. Your days, your nights. Your joy and laughter and even the challenges and struggles. You make hell bearable, Bella Sanders."

It was too much. The sincerity in his voice, the slow almost agonizing way he filled me. The knowledge that this was it, the last time I'd get to be with him. That he was making the ultimate sacrifice so I could go home to my children.

I shattered. Clutching him tightly I screamed and screamed and screamed.

It wasn't until the release faded that the other screams registered. At first I thought they were echoes. The cries weren't ones of pleasure but pure terror. Followed by a high-pitched keening roar.

"The Bane," Declan gasped. "It's here."

CHAPTER 19
DONNA

"So, it's like a restaurant built into the back of a vehicle", I explained to Demon-Dad as I talked about Axel's desire to open a food truck and how I was helping him with it. "Although if Declan is staying behind I guess we're going to need another financial backer."

Demon-Dad nodded, though I wasn't sure how much of what I was saying made sense to him. Did he remember what a restaurant was? Or a vehicle? It seemed rude to ask and talking kept my wonky brain off the inevitable. "It just sucks though, you know? Bella deserves to be happy. And I've seen Declan with her babies. He'd be a great step-demon."

"I'm sorry," Demon-Dad said.

So was I. "You and Mom. Me and Axel. Now Bella and Declan. Are all Sanders women cursed when it comes to finding forever relationships?"

I glanced in the direction I'd seen Bella and Declan head a little while before. My heart was breaking for the two of them. They'd been growing closer and the more she felt for Declan, the more Bella fought it. Witnessing her slow fall had been the highlight of these past few months.

Demon-Dad opened his mouth, but a tremendous screech filled the arena.

"The Bane!" Someone shrieked. Demons scattered.

Something huge swept into the arena. "It can fly?" I gasped as the shadow of its wings passed over us. Bad enough when I'd thought it was just a lumbering threat, but it was airborne.

"Oh goddess, Bella!" I took off in a sprint in the direction the demon had escorted my sister.

"Donna, look out!" Demon-Dad tackled me from behind. Air exploded from my lungs as I hit the rocky ground with his weight on top of me. The rockface I'd been standing against exploded as a massive tentacle hit the rock with monstrous force.

Demon-Dad rolled off me. I lay there for a moment, fighting to regain my breath. Then I looked over at him. The shirt he'd been wearing was in tatters and stained with crimson. Several long spikes, like porcupine quills stuck out of his ruined chest.

"No," I crawled to him, only to see him cough up more blood. "Goddess, no." I pressed my hands against the wounds, careful not to touch the quills, and applied pressure. The contact made him flinch and didn't go a long way to keeping his blood in his body.

"Donna!" Bella shouted.

I glanced around, hunting for her in the chaos of running demons and the roaring creature that had been drawn to all of us in one place. "Here! Hurry, Dad's hurt."

I spotted her then, her long dark silver-streaked hair a wild tangle of love knots, and Declan by her side.

They stood across the arena from us and had just taken their first step toward us when a brilliant blue light appeared above their heads.

"The portal!" I shouted. Axel had done it. All that blue? That was the sky from Earth.

Demons caught sight of the open portal and made a break for it. The Bane landed and followed after them, spiny tentacles flailing.

The runes Bella had drawn were a few feet from where we'd gone down. They began to glow, pulsating with a crimson light.

My jaw dropped in horror as first the demons and then the monster were drawn up into the portal like being trapped in the suction of a giant vacuum.

Bella and Declan pressed themselves into the wall of the arena and skirted around the portal, picking their way carefully to us. Bella reached us first and fell to her knees, heedless of the impact on her poor joints.

"Help him," I looked up to Declan.

His expression grim, the dark-haired demon murmured, "There's nothing I can do. The Bane's spines are toxic."

"We just sent that thing to Shadow Cove," I cried, imagining Devon, lying there helpless in the sleeping spell while that awful creature stalked him.

All worries about what was happening back home faded as I stared down at Demon-Dad. His color had grown waxy, and all the heat was leeching out of him along with the blood.

"I'll hold it open," Demon-Dad muttered. "For as long as I can."

"What?" I breathed. "No. No. You're coming with us. You're going to meet your grandchildren...."

I'd been building it up in my head, I realized. All the living I wanted to do with him. I'd pictured him at Devon's graduation, and the grand opening of Axel's food truck.

My eventual wedding.

"Go, Donna. You aren't cursed. Neither is your sister. Go and be happy with your fury. Go now." He coughed and then tugged the shadow stone necklace until the string broke. He pushed it into my hand. "There isn't much time."

"We need to get back," Bella said. "Donna, the town's still asleep. They're completely defenseless."

And Axel was there. He'd gotten my message and done what I'd asked, opened the portal.

Castles in the sand. That's what my wonky brain had built. Dreams that would be washed away.

"I'm glad to have met you. Both of you." Demon-Dad whispered. "And I am...so proud of the women you've become."

"I'm sorry," Bella said and then tugged at me, yanking me, dragging me toward the portal.

I didn't fight, but neither did I help. Too lost in my imagination of the way it was supposed to be. I clutched his shadow stone in my fist.

Then tugging grew more insistent. Not Bella. It was

the portal that pulled on me, on all of us. My last sight was Demon-Dad, crawling toward the runes that would shut the portal and seal off the demon realm for good.

He raised a bloody hand in farewell. And then we were gone.

~

Bella

WE LANDED on the muddy front lawn of Storm Grove, several hundred yards from the manor, with a jarring thud. I stared up at the evergreens and the puffy white clouds that scudded across the blue sky. Heard the wind-chimes blowing in the breeze.

A hand grasped mine. I turned to Declan. His heart was in his flaming eyes as he focused on me. He was here, alive and whole. He drew in a deep breath and held it like a man who'd been given a reprieve. I squeezed his hand and brought it to my lips.

"Donna?" I gasped and pushed myself upright. "Donna!"

"Witchling. Over there." Declan pointed toward the tree line.

I pivoted in the direction he'd indicated and spied several unconscious bodies. Donna lay in the middle of them, curled into a ball.

I staggered to my feet and stumbled toward her just as the Bane shrieked again. Declan pulled me close and teleported to Donna's side.

She was breathing, thank the goddess, but her eyes

were closed, and her hair was matted on one side. She winced when I touched the area. "I think she hit her head."

"It was a rough landing," the demon agreed. "Hurry up. Let's get everyone indoors."

"Poppet!" Clyde called when I approached, my arm around my sister's waist. Declan, being used to magic on the mortal plane, was transporting the demons down to the werewolf bunkhouse. "It's good to see you. But what happened to your sister?"

"It's a long story, Clyde. Where's Axel?"

"He went off into the forest a little bit ago. Ah, here he comes now."

I turned and stepped back from the doorway in time to see Axel's fury form swoop through the sky, making a beeline for the house.

"What's that thing you brought back with you?" Bonnie asked. "It doesn't look friendly."

"It's not. Do me a favor and keep it on Storm Grove property."

"Consider it done, Poppet." The gargoyles flew off.

"Don!" Axel had spotted us. His back winged, slowing his descent and magic rippled over him between one step and the next until he appeared wholly human once more.

"The twins?" I gripped his arm with my free hand, almost dropping Donna. "Where are Astrid and Ember?"

He caught my sister and held her to him as though she were the most precious thing in the world.

"With Matilda Longshanks and Devon at her place. I

didn't want them here while we're fucking around with portals. What was that thing?"

"The demons call it a Bane," I told him as he swung Donna up into his arms. "It showed up right before you opened the portal and got sucked through. What are the chances you can kill it?"

Axel carried Donna through the atrium to the sofa in the living room and laid her across it. "I don't know. It's fast and I'm not sure if we have anything that would penetrate its hide. I had a sword, and it broke off when I tried to stab it."

I paced the living room before the fireplace which was still covered with a drop cloth. "Okay, so we can't transport it elsewhere." Having just sealed off the demon realm, I wasn't about to open another portal.

Declan appeared in my path, his hands wrapping around my forearms. "Easy, witchling."

I swayed into him, glad that even though our escape hadn't been the clean getaway I'd wanted, at least he was still here. "Did you secure all the demons?"

"They're with the werewolves. I thought it best until we defeat the Bane."

A smile tugged at the corners of my mouth. "You're so sure we can defeat it?"

He raised my hand to his lips. "You can do anything, witchling. If only you believe in yourself."

I swallowed hard. I'd been lured by demon magic, which had caused more problems than I wanted because I believed my magic had failed me when I needed it most. But the truth was, no magic in the world would solve every problem.

I frowned and pulled out of his grip. "Remember what you told me at the archives? That you knew you weren't stronger or faster, but you still won because you were clever. That's what we need to be—smarter than our opponent. Tell me everything you know about the Bane. Who created it? What does it subsist on when it can't get demon?"

"It's been part of the realm since its inception," Declan began. "Though there were once hundreds of us, the Bane can go days without feeding at all. And it feeds on memory."

"Like the demon realm," I nodded.

"A little. It eats flesh too. Some of the ancient demons speculated that it was our jailer and it fed on memories to weaken demons and make them easier to catch."

I stopped, my heart pounding. What was it Donna had said when I'd wanted to destroy the demon plane?

Let's get out of here before we nuke the place.

"You said that the Bane can go days without feeding at all. But it's in our world now. What if we overfeed it?"

Declan's dark brows drew together. "I'm not sure I understand."

I waved toward the window. "Billions of us with billions upon billions of memories, thoughts, dreams. So, let's let it gorge on dreams."

"Whose dreams?" Axel asked.

I considered it a moment. "Shadow Cove. They're all sleeping so it will be easy enough to harvest their dreams along with the memories of the hallucinations. We can collect them if you can deliver them and make sure the Bane eats them."

"I can do it," Axel's jaw set in a stubborn line.

"Me too," a soft voice said from the couch.

I turned to see Donna's eyes were open. "Good to see you, sis. We really could use your help."

Axel crouched beside her once more. "Hey, Don. Welcome back."

She covered his hand with hers. "You got my message."

He brought her knuckles to his lips and kissed them softly.

I couldn't let Donna do it alone. Too many times my sister had gone out of her way to save me from my mistakes and been hurt or almost killed in the process. "We'll all do it. We're stronger together."

An ear-splitting screech echoed through the house.

Donna's gaze drifted toward the ceiling. "Let's hope we're strong enough."

CHAPTER 20
DONNA

Bella and Declan had disappeared into her bedroom, presumably to get started on the spell to gather dreams. Axel remained crouched on the floor in front of me, his gray eyes worried.

"You okay, babe?" he murmured as he tucked some hair behind my ear.

The shadow stone necklace was still clutched in my hand. My eyes stung as I fought back tears. "I met my dad. He didn't make it though."

"I'm sorry." Axel drew me off the couch and into his arms. "What was he like?"

I buried my face in his shirt. He smelled of laundry detergent and ozone. Classic Axel. "Like Devon. And like me. Kinda ADHD hyper. But a good guy." One who had made the ultimate sacrifice, so my twin and I had a shot at happily ever after.

I hadn't known him for long, but he'd carved a special place in my heart.

Axel held me to him. I didn't cry. There would be time

to mourn Demon-Dad later. Finally, I pulled back from him and said, "If you leave again, I'm going with you."

Lightning flashed in those eyes. "Don, it's dangerous."

I covered his lips with my fingertips. "No arguments. I won't fight about this. The twins are getting older, and Bella has Declan. I'm a fifth wheel here without you. If you think it's too dangerous to be around family, fine. But I'm going to be with you no matter what."

His throat bobbed and then he leaned down and pressed his lips lightly against mine.

"Hey, you two," Bella called from the doorway. "Could you come and give us a hand?"

Axel pulled back and it wasn't until I lowered my hand from his face that I realized exactly how grubby I was. "Ick. I need a bath."

"I'll help you with that, later," Axel grinned, and my heart pounded. Goddess, it was good to have something to look forward to again.

Bella rolled her eyes, but I caught her smile as she pivoted on her heel and stalked into her bedroom.

"What's all this?" I spied the glowing green stones spread out over the bedspread. "It looks like the rocks from the demonic plane?"

"That's because they are rocks from the demonic plane." Declan stood before the windows. He'd doffed his leather coat, and his sleeves were rolled up. I'd never seen him look so relaxed. I could only imagine what he'd look like if we weren't about to battle a monster from the underworld. "Shadow Stones."

"We know the Shadow Stones can pull memories,"

Bella explained as she set to work tying knots in red string. "Each knot represents the mind of someone in Shadow Cove. What I want to pull are all the memories from right before we put them to sleep as well as their dreams. That way they can wake up and think it was a gas leak or some other mundane nonsense."

"Good planning," I nodded. "Where do you need me?"

She nodded toward another ball of string. "Help me tie the knots. Speak the spell, you will release what no longer serves you, and let it serve us."

I did as she asked, my hands falling into a rhythm.

"I'm going out to patrol with Bonnie and Clyde," Axel put a hand on my shoulder.

"Be careful," I leaned into his touch, the warmth that radiated from him. He kissed my filthy cheek and then flew out the open window.

Declan stirred the pot in silence. All his focus was on creating the potion that would seal

the dreams into the strings.

"What if this isn't enough?" I hissed to Bella. "What if we don't kill the Bane?"

She met my gaze and held it. "Let's hope it is enough."

I tied the next knot. And hoped.

Bella

AXEL FLEW BACK through the window just as I was tying the last knot. "It's heading this

way."

"Is it ready?" I asked Declan.

The demon nodded. "As it will ever be."

Donna and I set our knots aside and then began collecting the stones. One by one we dropped them into the potion. Then followed with the knotted strings.

"That's it?" Donna asked.

I nodded and stepped back. Despite what I'd said, I was worried the memories from Shadow Cove dreamers wouldn't be enough. What if we didn't even slow the Bane down?

Declan met my gaze and the fire burned brighter in his eyes as he murmured, "We've got this."

We. Not only me. Not Donna. All of us. Together.

Axel and Declan carried the cauldron between them out the front door. Donna slipped her hand into mine and squeezed tight.

I squeezed back and then turned my gaze to look toward the sky. A moment later the boom of great wings proceeded an ear-splitting screech. Bonnie and Clyde swooped into view, their paths crisscrossing as they sailed over the house.

Then the Bane appeared, its hideous maw open.

"Ready!" I called.

Declan nodded even as the Bane's head pivoted in our direction.

"Aim!" I ordered.

Declan waved his hands at the bubbling cauldron. It levitated several feet off the ground.

Axel spread his wings and crouched down low.

Heartbeat. Heartbeat. Heartbeat. I waited until the Bane opened its beak to shriek once more.

"Fire!" I shouted.

Axel lept. I couldn't see him. He moved between the span of heartbeats. One moment he was there, the next he and the cauldron were nowhere in sight.

"Bullseye!" Declan crowed.

The Bane was flapping its wings frantically. Its head shook from side to side.

"Uh oh," Donna said. "Bella?"

I saw it too. The Bane was on a collision course with the house.

And the three fools standing right in front of it.

Smoke engulfed me at the same moment strong arms drew me to him. I couldn't see as Declan teleported us well out of the way.

"Donna!" I called out. "Did you get her?"

"Axel did." Declan pointed as the smoke dissipated. I spotted my sister and Axel up in the sky. Her green eyes practically bugged out of her head.

"We got it?" I looked to where the Bane had crashed into the side of the manor, taking out the conservatory and part of the newly remodeled kitchen as well. "Is it dead?"

More smoke cleared as well as dust and debris from the impact.

My heart sank when I heard the familiar cry. "It didn't work." It hadn't been enough.

"We slowed it down considerably. See how it's struggling to rise? Just a little more...." His voice trailed off as he glanced again at Donna and Axel. "Wait here, witch-ling. I have an idea."

Before I could protest, the smoke surrounded him once more.

Leaving me on the ground. Alone. Facing the disoriented Bane.

~

Donna

DECLAN APPEARED in the air beside us.

"What are you doing?" I shouted to the demon.

He didn't respond. Instead, he pulled something out from beneath the collar of his shirt. I spotted a flash of green and then his hand closed around it.

"What is that?" Axel frowned as Declan held it out to him.

"You need to feed it more," Declan's flaming gaze was focused on Axel. "Whatever you have to spare."

"What?" I glanced from the demon to Axel and back. "What are you talking about?"

Axel's brows pulled together, and he reached for the necklace. "How?"

"Make a bargain," the demon said with a smile. "The same way you did with me to get those powers in the first place."

I shook my head, unable to believe for a second what I was hearing.

"*You?* You're the one that made him a fury?"

"Made him reincarnate as a fury," Declan corrected. "Just as Gunther wished."

The Bane screeched as it fought its way free of the rubble and Bella screamed, "Whatever the hell you're doing, hurry!"

"Take care of them," Axel transferred me in midair between himself and the demon.

"What?" I reached for him, but the demon held me tight.

"Always," Declan nodded to him.

My heart was pounding so hard I worried I'd pass out. The Bane shrieked again and snapped its jaws toward Bella. She scrambled back out of the way.

"The life I don't want for all of ours." Axel gripped the stone in his hand.

"Wait? What?" I reached for him, needing to cling to him, to shake him until he told me what was happening. My gut clenched around an icy ball of fear.

Axel dove. Down down down. On a collision course with the Bane.

"It's a bargain well struck," the demon murmured at the point of impact.

With a green flash, the Bane screamed once more, and then....

They were gone.

∽

Bella

THE COLLISION KNOCKED me back on my ass in the dirt. I threw my hand over my face to protect it from flying debris. I needn't have bothered. When I glanced up, Declan stood beside me and had erected a transparent shield around the three of us. I knew because Donna was pounding on the thing, like the world's most hysterical mime.

"Axel!" She was screaming his name over and over.

"You all right, witchling?" Declan asked as he helped me to my feet.

"Not sure." I shook my head from side to side and then looked out at the chaos that used to be part of the manor. "What just happened?"

"Axel fed the Bane," Donna screeched.

"Fed it what?"

"His fury," Declan said.

"What?" Donna and I rounded on him.

Declan sighed. "It was the only thing I could think of. Furies live hundreds of years, longer and richer lives than demons."

"Axel's only a few decades old!" Donna threw herself at Declan, who caught her by the arms before she could strike him.

"Yes, but the fury I merged his soul with was hundreds of years old," The demon explained patiently. "Gunther was my very first bargain, the one that consigned me and my mother to the demonic realm."

I let out an audible breath and then looked back to the wreckage. "So, you basically fed the Bane Gunther and his fury self?"

"Axel did. Hold your sister, witchling so I can go see if there's anything left of the man."

Donna froze. "He's alive?"

"Well let's hope so." Declan lowered the bubble and then strode forward. I held onto Donna who held herself still as though she was afraid if she moved too fast, she would come apart at the seams. Declan crouched down and began shoving rubble aside. He dug down and grasped something.

Donna sobbed as Axel was pulled free of the wreckage, coughing, dusty but very much alive. She broke free of my hold and sprinted for him, throwing herself against him with enough force that they both landed on the ground in a tangle of dusty limbs.

"It's gone?" Axel shook his head as though dazed. "It's really gone?"

"Don't you ever do that to me again," Donna pounded on him. She was either laughing or sobbing. Hard to tell which.

I looked up at Declan. "Was that the memory you carried in your stone?"

He nodded once. "To remind me that some things are worth the price."

I sighed and leaned into him. "Damn it, demon. Will you ever stop surprising me?"

He kissed the top of my head. "I'll make you a bargain witchling."

"Oh, no." I shook my head. "No way. No bargains. I've learned my lesson."

"Pity," Declan said. "And here I was going to make you rich."

I met his burning gaze and held it. "I have everything I could ever want."

"Make him at least fix the house though," Donna called out.

"And invest in my food truck!" Axel added. "I'll even name all the items on the menu after him. Demon's delight chicken wings."

Declan grimaced. Then frowned. "I don't think I've had chicken wings."

"Then you're in for a treat." I nestled in close to my demon. "Even if you can't bargain with me, it sounds like you have a few other takers."

"Foolish mortals," Declan shook his head. "Will they ever learn?"

I nudged him in the ribs. "Come on, demon. Let's go get our children."

His smile was pure delight. "We can get them ice cream. I still have a dozen flavors left to try."

"Whatever you want, big guy," I said as we headed around the house. "Whatever makes you happy."

"That would be you, witchling. Forever and always."

I looked up at him and breathed, "It's a bargain well struck."

EPILOGUE

Donna

4 Months Later

"Today's the day!" I bounced out of bed and headed for the hook on the back of the door reaching for my bathrobe. "Come on sleepyhead. Get a move on."

Axel groaned and threw an arm up over his face. "Don, it's not even light out."

I couldn't help admiring the bulge of muscles in his arms and bare chest. "You don't need light to get cooking."

"We're not even open until noon. Come back to bed." That arm that I'd been admiring reached for me.

My teeth sank into my lower lip. Tempting. As always. Everything about Axel was tempting, always had been. At first, I'd been worried that being set free of the fury within would have changed him. He'd realize how many options he had and wouldn't want the same things he'd wanted before. Like his soon-to-be forty-six-year-old girlfriend.

I should have known better. Because it wasn't the fury that made Axel loyal to me, it was his nature.

"I'm taking a shower," I announced. "You want to join me?"

The hand lowered and he narrowed those gray eyes at me. There were times when I missed the flashes of lightning. Nothing but a clear, enticing gray, like a calm sea, looked out at me now.

"You drive a hard bargain, lady."

I shrugged and opened the bedroom door. "I learned from the best." With that I sauntered into the hall, shutting the door in his face.

It was too early for our lodgers to be up. Demons, like high school kids, were often late sleepers. Instead of the gothic B&B that Declan had once envisioned, we now ran a halfway house for demons who were still dealing with all the effects of their transition. Most days were pure chaos. I loved every second of it.

I'd just stepped under the spray when the bathroom door opened. Axel slipped inside. I presented him with my back, my smile victorious as the shower curtain squealed and then his hands were on me, caressing me, loving me, in a way only he could.

It wasn't only the change in occupation that lifted my spirits.

Axel toweled me off, starting with my hair. He looked

207

much less sleepy and was more enthusiastic about what lay ahead. "You're going to be there?"

"As soon as I pick up Devon." I put my hand on his face. "You know I wouldn't miss your grand opening."

He nuzzled my hand. "It wouldn't have happened without you, you know that, right?"

When I nodded, he kissed my palm and then reached for a towel. "Bella's coming too. And the twin terrors?"

"Of course. They just got in from the coast last night." I hadn't expected them to come to Storm Grove, but the Demon had appeared, looking like a pack mule loaded down with diaper bags, and luggage and looking as pleased with punch."

"Took you long enough, Donna Sanders-Allen," he'd sniffed. "I like to set a uniform standard for all my lodgings. Making guests wait on the doorstep is abhorrently rude."

"You're not the boss of me, Declan." I planted my hands on my hips and lifted my chin, completely unimpressed with his threats. "They are."

I gestured to where Bella was chasing after the twins who were running as fast as their chubby little legs could carry them.

Bella had let it slip that the Demon had transferred ownership of Storm Grove to Ember and Astrid almost as soon as he'd gotten it. He and Bella were named as managers, though they rarely spent any time on the property. They were too busy traveling the world, their little family unit inseparable.

I'd never seen my sister so happy.

Now I made my way down to the newly remodeled

kitchen, admiring the ebony black cabinets and shining chrome fixtures, the black and silver stone countertop, and the ultramodern appliances that allowed Axel to work his magic. The coffee was already brewing, so I knew someone must be up. I found Declan, Astrid, and Ember out on the terrace that overlooked the lake. The twins were in their highchairs. Bowls of Cheerios with sliced strawberries sat on their tray. They were eating with their bare hands, much to the demon's chagrin.

"Savages. Don't you know that table manners are all that separates us from lower life forms?" He wiped Ember's sticky face with a wet washcloth.

"Dad looks good on you," I told him. "Where's Bells?"

The demon glanced up at me. "She went up to the cemetery, to pay her respects."

I nodded once. "Think I'll join her. Thanks for the coffee."

"Don't pollute it with all that crap you typically use!" Declan called after me. "It's a very expensive Peruvian blend!"

I tossed him a jaunty salute and went ahead to make two cups of coffee exactly the way I always did with cream and sugar before heading out the door and up the hill toward the Sanders family cemetery.

Bella stood barefoot before our mother's gravestone. I'd added a second marker to the left where I'd buried Demon Dad's necklace.

I waited by the gate while she paid her respects. Unlike Bella, I didn't feel the need to visit the cemetery every single day. I knew she felt guilty for leaving, even though she shouldn't. While she may be a Sanders legacy witch, that didn't mean she needed to live her life for the past and the wishes of our dead relatives.

She was working her way through the feelings. And I was proud of her for stretching herself to be the person she wanted to be instead of what she thought everyone else wanted her to be.

"Bless you," Bella murmured as she took the coffee mug I offered. "I haven't had any yet."

"You okay?" I asked as she looked around the grounds.

"Yeah. It's weird, being here after being gone for so long. You've made all these changes."

"Are you unhappy with them?" I asked.

"Not at all. I think it's great." She pointed over the hill toward the stables. "Horses at Storm Grove. Who'd have thunk it?"

"Working with them is great for the demons," I said. "And the stables bring in plenty of revenue. Between that and the apple orchard, the estate is finally paying for itself."

Bella let out a long, contented sigh. "Are you going to get Devon?"

"As soon as I finish my coffee." It was a six-hour round trip to his college and back and I needed to shake a leg to make sure we were back in time for Axel's big launch.

"Mind if I come with you?" Bella asked.

Her request surprised me. It shouldn't have though. The Bella from a year ago didn't do road trips for leisure. She'd changed so much in such a short amount of time.

"You're leaving the demon to babysit all day?" I asked.

She shrugged. "It's not babysitting when it's his kids. That's called parenting. Don't let him fool you, he loves it."

I laughed. "You're ride or mine?"

She gave me a level stare. "What do you think?"

"I think a dorm fridge and all of Devon's junk won't fit in the Deville."

Bella grinned. "Good thing I know a little magic. I'll snag the keys."

"And some shoes!" I called after her, then laughed when she flipped me the bird.

~

Bella

"Stop fidgeting," I told Donna as we waited for our turn to park in front of Declan's dormitory. All around us young adults were hugging parents, grandparents, siblings, and friends. People were shoving microwaves and athletic equipment into overfilled SUVs, dogs were sticking their noses out of windows to greet long-lost pack members.

"We should have brought Joseline," I murmured, and Donna snorted.

After waking from his enchanted sleep, Devon seemed eager to head back to school. There was no sign he recalled anything, not attacking his mother, not Axel's fury barreling down on him like a ton of bricks. He'd spent spring break with friends in Florida and had skipped coming home for Easter. With every missed visit Donna had grown antsier.

"I need to tell him," Donna muttered.

"Tell him what, exactly?" I wasn't against the idea at all. I asked to allow Donna time to sort through her emotions and come up with a plan of attack.

"All of it," she took a deep breath and then turned to face me. "What if he's a sleeper dud like I was? What if he suddenly manifests an ability at forty and I'm not around to answer his questions? He needs to know everything I know so he can be prepared for whatever lies ahead."

I cast her a sideways glance and admitted a long-held truth. "When I grow up, I want to be like you."

That startled her. "Really?"

I nodded. "You're the best mom in the universe. Always doing the right thing, even when it's the hard thing."

Her lips parted and her eyes misted.

I wagged a finger in her face. "Do not start crying. If you start, then I'll start, and your son will think we're emotionally unstable."

She sniffled and turned to the window. "Oh! There he is!" Donna pointed at the line where Devon stood, a massive pile of stuff looming over him and she grimaced "Oh man, it's worse than I thought."

"Don't worry, I've got this." I pulled out the shrinking charm that Declan had made for me. It made transporting the twin's gear a breeze.

Donna was too nervous to argue. I parked and waited

while she got out. There was a tense moment before Declan wrapped his arms around his mother's neck. I gave them their privacy, sending a quick text to Declan to let him know we'd made it to the school safely. My demon was a fretter and though ADHD often had me running on out-of-sight, out-of-mind capacity, I'd developed the habit of always texting before I got out of the car. Ritual wasn't just for witchcraft.

I exited the car and tilted my face up to the sun, basking in the glorious weather. Several sets of eyes focused on me, but I lifted my chin and circled the DeVille, so I could greet my nephew.

"Aunt Bella." He grinned at me. "Mom didn't say you were coming."

"Contrary to what she thinks, your mother doesn't know everything." I didn't demand a hug. Personal space and all that. "Is this everything or is there a storage unit we need to empty somewhere out on town?"

Devon laughed a little nervously. "It didn't seem like so much in my room."

"Don't sweat it, kid. The trunk on this baby is bigger than it looks." I muttered the incantation to activate the charm and then opened the trunk.

Everything fit, just as I knew it would. Devon's brows drew together as he watched his snowboard, his fridge, microwave, rug, oversized storage bins, and three months' worth of laundry disappear into the depths of the DeVille.

"Wow, okay, I didn't think that would work," Devon said as I slammed the trunk closed. "I better go tell Katie I won't need her to take anything."

"Katie?" Donna's spine stiffened. "Whose Katie?"

"It's a long story. I'll be right back."

I leaned against the DeVille beside my sister as we watched her son run up beside a petite brunette and murmur in her ear. "Dollars to doughnuts Katie was part of the reason for his mid-semester crisis. Or what brought him out of it."

Donna tucked some hair behind her ear. "Suddenly I feel nervous for an entirely different reason."

"Should we buy him condoms?" I asked.

My twin snorted. "Like we'll remember."

"Good point." I nudged her arm. "It'll be okay. He's going to get along famously with Axel. Their practically the same age."

"Shut up," Donna laughed. "And none of that in front of Devon. Demons and werewolves and a former fury who was my lover in a past life. This is going to be complicated enough to explain."

I lowered my sunglasses. Magic pulsed around me, and I knew she could see her reflection in my eyes. "Donna Sanders-Allen. You are a legacy witch. Complicated, you can handle."

Donna grinned and I felt the pulse of comeuppance that twined between our bodies. "And you know what, Bella Sanders? I predict that we're going to get everything that's coming to us."

Note from the author:
Make sure you've read the book first to avoid spoilers!

. . .

THANK you so much for taking this journey with me. Shadow Cove is a place full of secrets. The twists and turns in this series would not relent. True confession time. The Demon-Dad angle totally took me by surprise as well as the demon migration to the mortal plane. Expect to see them popping up in future stories.

I loved giving Declan and Bella a happily ever after. They've both come a very long way since book 1 even though their natures are still a wee bit shady. Just shows you that growth can happen even while people stay true to their nature. And Donna and Axel? Well, tell me they don't deserve a total win on every front.

So, what's next? Keep reading for a taste of the *Kitchen Witch Wedding* coming soon!

Love and light,

Jennifer L. Hart

P.S. Please consider leaving an honest review of this book. Reviews help readers like you find the kinds of books they love and keep writers like me behind the keyboard.

CRAVING MORE MIDLIFE MAGIC?

Thank you so much for reading. It's my honor to write about midlife heroines, especially with the blend of supernatural adventures and real-world struggles in paranormal women's fiction. And I couldn't do it without you.

Not ready to leave the witches and shifters community yet? Please visit authorjenniferlhart.com. I have written several short stories, exclusive for my newsletter subscribers. I would love to stay in touch with you.

Bonus content for newsletter subscribers includes:

- **"Fairy Wine. A Magical Midlife Misadventure"**. Gwen is recovering from an emotionally abusive ex and lacks the courage to live life on her own terms. Andreas is a fae prince in need of a new anchor, a human to tether him to the mortal plane. On the night

217

of the summer solstice, will they find love, only to lose it come dawn? Find out now!

- **"Midlife Passions and Predators."** Valentine's Day on the OBX. Takes place a few weeks after the end of *Midlife Shift and Shenanigans*. John and Jessica have some news that's going to rock Sam's world. Can Mathis and Damien help her overcome the shock and show her that change can sometimes be a blessing in disguise?

- **Which Witch to Alaska** Maeve and Kal take a trip to Alaska for a wedding. Book 3.5 in the Silver Sisters series.

Sign up now at <u>authorjenniferlhart.com</u>.

SAMPLE FROM KITCHEN WITCH WEDDING

"Oh please, Brittney. You wouldn't know a good time if you were sitting on its face," my sister Emma slurred and then promptly slid off the barstool. The patrons of *McGuffins* didn't turn a hair. There weren't too many places in Crestmont where a soul could go to get rip-roaring drunk. Up until the 1980's the town had been a dry county, and while places like the country club served wine or craft beers, *McGuffins* was about the only place that served hard liquor.

Nope, they were all too busy watching the football game on TV.

Maybe I would have been more concerned for her if I hadn't been budgeting my energy bucks all week for our outing. Sisterly bonding and all that rot. I'd been careful to shower that morning, so the temperature shift didn't trigger an MS attack. I'd paced myself all day, eating protein and taking my meds, resting at periodic intervals. And when I'd arrived, Emma had been well past sloshed and on her way to black-out drunk.

The shot glasses Emma had emptied sat upside down on the battle-scarred oak bar in front of her, lined up like good little soldiers.

So much for girl's night out.

I rooted around in the saddle bags attached to my wheelchair until I found my phone and scrolled through the contacts. Someone half my age and autoimmune disease free would have found the number in half the time. MS was a game changer though. It slowed down my motor functions to a crawl and everything I did was deliberate.

My sister's fiancé, Tyler, answered on the first ring. "You okay, Brittney?"

Despite the crappy situation, I smiled at the concern in his voice. Taylor was one of the good ones and not just because he was a police officer. "Yeah, but I need a hand with Emma. She sort of...." I trailed off as I cocked my head and studied my sister's inert form. "Melted."

"Melted huh? Like the wicked witch of the South?"

"That was the West," I corrected, though I made no comments about witches. Even though Taylor was going to be family soon, there were some things better left in the broom closet. "Bottom line is she's passed out on the floor."

"I'll be there in ten." Tyler hung up.

I stowed my phone and then gestured to Mike, the bartender.

He sauntered over, slinging the bar towel over his shoulder in a move I was sure he'd practiced in the mirror. "Can I get you something?"

"A vodka cranberry, please, Mike."

"Really?" A pimple peaked beneath the patchy white-blond stubble that Mike was trying to grow in but was turning out to be more of a neck beard. "I've never seen you drink."

"That's because I don't." Booze plus MS meds weren't a good combination. My usual method for combating stress was dark chocolate ganache. Emma's comment about me not knowing how to have a good time stung and I didn't have any cake to help me over the hump. Besides, vodka, if done well, didn't taste like anything. I even used it in ice cream sometimes, to thicken the soft serve.

At his raised brow I explained, "Special occasion. We're celebrating the big game," I pointed to the TV where one oversized galoot was sacking another. Or was that tackling? I could never tell the difference.

Mike glanced down to where Emma snored. Then he shrugged and moved down the bar to pour my drink. While his back was turned, I checked to make sure no one was watching. Then using the come to me spell, I floated Emma's wallet out of her coat pocket. It wasn't fair that Tyler had to pick up her bar tab as well as her drunk carcass.

Mike leaned over the bar to hand me my drink. I forked over my sister's Visa and saluted him. Then with nothing better to do, I turned my attention to the TV.

Football and I had a long, sordid history. In high school I'd been forced to go to the bonfires and Home-coming dances. "It will help you fit in," Mom had told me. "In the South it's all about family and football."

She'd been trying to help me break free of my shell.

I'd been the goth girl, the weird one with no friends. My only hobby was food, the kitchen the only place I felt normal. Little did she know her insistence only got me bullied.

I was nursing my second drink when Tyler strode in wearing his uniform. I winced. I hadn't realized he was on duty.

"You're not gonna lock her up in the drunk tank, are you?" I asked. "I was pissed at her but not that pissed."

"Nah." He patted me on the shoulder in greeting than bent down and scooped Emma up off the floor and slung her over his shoulder in a Fireman's carry. "You need a lift, Brittney?"

Gesturing to my chair I said, "Think I'm fine to drive this sweet ride. Thanks though."

He dipped his head and then turned, my sister hanging limply over his back like a human stole.

Mike handed me back Emma's card, which I signed with a shaky X. Fine motor skills, like writing, were the toughest to keep a handle on. Of course, my large motor skills weren't too great either, hence the wheelchair. Once again, my attention drifted to the TV as two men collided with the force of battering rams.

"Idiots," I breathed. Didn't they know how fragile the human body was? What a delicate and breakable machine they inhabited? All the money in the world couldn't buy a soul another home if their physical being was wrecked beyond repair.

"Great game, huh?" Mike leaned on the sticky bar top that he should have been wiping down.

"Freaking fabulous." I knocked back my drink and then turned my wheelchair and headed out into the night.

Screw vodka. I needed chocolate.

Coming soon!

Made in the USA
Monee, IL
10 October 2024

67570191R00134